Would Jamie's nightmare ever end?

"What's going on around here?" Ben Wheelock demanded. "What are you doing back here, Braxton?"

"Ben!" Jamie cried in relief.

As Chad turned slowly around, he pulled a small pistol from inside of his shirt.

Ben looked down at the pistol. "Have you gone mad?"

"Shut up!" A smile spread over Chad's face. "How good of you to stop by and lend us a hand." He grabbed Jamie and moved away from Ben. "Give me all the pills you've got. You know what I mean."

"I'll give you whatever you want, just let Jamie go."

"No!" Chad hissed. "She's coming with me."

Ben hesitated. He looked at Jamie. She was shaking with fear. "Let her go!"

"Don't make me angry, Wheelock!"

"Ben, please, just do as he says," whispered Jamie.

The pharmacist took two keys from his pocket and reluctantly unlocked the cabinets. He removed two bottles of pills. Chad grabbed them and in one quick motion hit Ben on the head with the butt of the pistol. Ben fell to the floor. He wasn't moving.

"No!" Jamie screamed.

Chad je_____ith the gun.

"Be qui

KJERSTI HOFF BAEZ is the author of two children's books, *Corrie ten Boom* and *Ruth*, of the best-selling Young Reader's Christian Library series as well as inspirational romances. A mother of three, Mrs. Baez finds time as well to write book reviews for *Virtue* magazine.

Passage
of the Heart

Kjersti Hoff Baez

Heartsong Presents

ISBN 1-55748-355-8

PASSAGE OF THE HEART

PRINTED IN U.S.A.

one

Jamie squinted at the midwinter sun and pulled her sweater tighter around her slim shoulders.

"I should've worn my coat," she murmured. "Grandma's going to throw a fit when she sees me without it."

The January air was appropriately cold. An occasional gust of wind reminded the young woman she was no longer in California. The rolling foothills of the Catskills surrounded the tiny train station liked a rumpled quilt.

Jamie sighed. She was really here. Her father's speech still echoed in her mind: "You've got no discipline. You're hanging around with the wrong crowd. Arrested twice for drunken behavior, and now you've flunked out of college."

Her parents had given her two choices: Go to community college and live at home (under their rules), or spend a year with Grandma Kate. "Maybe Grandma's principles will rub off on you," Dad had said.

Jamie rolled her eyes at the thought of staying at home. After being away at school for two years (well, almost two), she wasn't about to endure the humiliation of living with Mom and Dad. And community college! She rolled her eyes again. Staying with Grandma Kate wouldn't be much better, but at least she'd be away from home.

Running her fingers through her rich brown hair, Jamie straightened her shoulders. "Besides," she said aloud, "I'm almost twenty-two. I don't need Mom and Dad breathing down my neck."

"Here, here!" said a deep voice behind her. Startled, she turned around and came face to chest with what looked like an overgrown cowboy. Looking up, she saw two pale blue eyes twinkling down at her. She gulped.

"You certainly are the picture of independence," he grinned.

"Uh, ahem, I uh . . ." Jamie realized how idiotic she must look, shivering like a child with several suitcases cluttering the platform at her feet.

"You must be Jamie Carrigan. Mrs. K couldn't come for you on account of her car not working so she sent me. My name is Judah."

He held out his hand to welcome her to Caderville, but Jamie was reluctant to respond. She didn't like feeling idiotic, and this tall oaf made her feel like a fool. She made up her mind she wasn't going to like him.

"Thanks for the fanfare," the young woman said sarcastically, "but could you please just take me to my grandmother's? I'm tired and I'm freezing."

"It's no wonder. Where's your coat?" The man didn't wait for an answer but reached down to pick up her suitcases. He loaded her belongings into a beat-up red truck. Jamie followed in silence and climbed into the cab.

Judah threw the truck into gear and they made their way through the small town of Caderville. He rambled on about what a wonderful person Mrs. King was and what a great man Mr. King had been, but Jamie wasn't listening.

"Where in the world did you get a name like Judah?" she interrupted. "Sounds like something out of the Middle Ages."

"Actually, it's found in the Bible, ma'am."

"I know. I wasn't born yesterday, for Pete's sake." She sighed in disgust. Hopefully she wouldn't have anything to do with this guy after he dropped her off at Grandma's. "So why'd your parents give you a name like that?"

"Well, ma'am, actually my parents didn't name me. I was found in a box on the steps of Hillside Church on a Sunday morning. The sermon that day happened to be about the Lion of Judah so the pastor's wife named me Judah. She and the reverend adopted me."

"Oh."

Touché, Jamie thought to herself. *Instant replay of me playing idiot. I think I'll keep my mouth shut.* She settled into her seat, determined to keep quiet.

Through the window of the old truck, Jamie reacquainted herself with the terrain of her mom's home state. The naked trees colored the hills pewter, and bands of evergreen crested the tops with a dark forest green. She caught glimpses of the river, a silver ribbon that flowed through the valley. Whenever Ellen Carrigan spoke of her childhood home, it was with real tenderness. "Must be heaven overflowed one day and a piece of it settled down in the Delaware Valley," she would say. Jamie had to admit the foothills did have a beauty of their own.

Caderville was nestled in the valley and was scarcely big enough to call a town. The well-preserved buildings that lined Main Street greeted Jamie like an entourage of friendly old faces. She studied each one carefully to see if anything had changed.

Oh, wow, a movie theater, she said lamely to herself.

Judah broke the silence as if he had read her mind.

"It's new," he said pointing to the theater. "A man from New York moved up here and renovated the old Macintosh building. Caused a lot of excitement."

"Yes, how terribly exciting," said Jamie. "Where I come from, we have five theaters."

Judah whistled and shook his head in disbelief.

"Who would want to go the movies that often?" he asked.

Jamie looked at him in sheer amazement. *He's from the Stone Ages. I just know it. Somehow an alien ship transported him from the age of the dinosaur and dropped him in the twentieth century. Why Caderville?* she thought. *Why me?*

"What do you do for excitement?" she asked. "Watch the grass grow? Catch wart toads and have frog races?"

Judah smiled. "Mostly I work," he said. "But there are plenty of fascinating things to do around here, if you look. And I do have some hobbies I enjoy."

Let me guess, thought Jamie. *You rope grasshoppers, sit around a campfire, and count the stars.*

She looked at the dark haired, blue-eyed, Neanderthal cowboy. The less she knew about him the better, so she dropped the conversation. Hopefully she wouldn't run into him very often while she stayed at Grandma Kate's.

Judah turned the truck down a dirt road and drove a mile out of town. A mailbox with King painted on it in red letters stood resolutely at the head of a long driveway. Jamie turned to look at the sloping yard and old farm house. Despite the fact that only boredom awaited her in Caderville, it was always nice to visit Grandma Kate. There was something comforting about her that Jamie couldn't explain.

Snow graced the yard with a sweeping whiteness that dazzled Jamie's eyes. The white house with the black shutters bid welcome to Jamie, saluting her with a customary wisp of smoke from the chimney. Jamie knew that meant a fire in the fireplace and cocoa in a mug.

"Stop the truck," she exclaimed to its driver, momentarily forgetting to act like an adult. He obeyed and she leapt from the truck, running through the ankle-deep snow. She raced toward the house as another, younger Jamie had often raced. Young woman met with child, and with one burst of excitement, Jamie reached the front door with its iron clacker. The red door flew open, and there stood Katherine King.

"Grandma!" Jamie shouted, grabbing the woman in a bear hug.

"Good heavens, Jamie, you'll break my neck!" Kate protested with a smile. "And where in the world is your coat?" She held her granddaughter at arm's length. "Have you lost your mind? It's January, dear. Around here that means snow, cold. Or have you forgotten?"

Jamie sighed. "Oh, Grandma. It's in my suitcase."

"Well at least you brought it!" she exclaimed. "My how you've grown. Why, you're a beautiful young woman! Even prettier than the pictures you sent me!"

"Oh Grandma," Jamie blushed and walked through the foyer to the living room. A fire was crackling cheerfully in the large, stone fireplace. Jamie hurried over to enjoy the warmth. She let the heat from the fire soothe away the cold in her hands and feet. Then she flopped down on the green, overstuffed sofa in front of the fireplace.

"This is great," she sighed happily. "I'm so glad to be here." Her earlier misgivings disappeared, chased away by the comfort of her grandmother's home.

"And I'm glad you're here! I'm glad Judah was able to

pick you up. Let me give you a proper introduction." She turned to call to him, but he was gone. Jamie's suitcases were assembled neatly in the foyer.

"I don't know how he does that," Kate said, half to herself. She looked out through the open door and caught a glimpse of red as Judah's truck bounded out the driveway. "Here one minute and gone the next."

Jamie let go a sigh of relief. *Goodbye and good riddance*, she said to herself.

"Come and have some dinner," Kate called to Jamie from the kitchen. "Then we'll see about getting you settled in your room."

Jamie pulled herself away from the comfortable sofa and followed her grandmother into the big country kitchen. The aroma of roast beef and gravy tantalized Jamie's appetite. She sat down across from her grandmother and fingered the lace tablecloth that covered the table with soft whiteness.

Kate smiled at her granddaughter and bowed her head to say grace. Jamie bowed her head too, but she didn't hear the heartfelt prayer of thanks for food and family. Her mind wandered to the prospect of spending a whole year in the boondocks. She glanced over at her grandmother. *As long as she doesn't try pushing her God stuff on me we'll be fine*, she thought. *Maybe this year won't be so bad.*

A firm "Amen" tugged Jamie back to the table. As the two women enjoyed their meal together, evening stole silently into the valley. Faint pink reflected on the snow as the sun fell behind the hills. The blue of evening took its place. Muffled laughter rested lightly in the night air, a token of life from within the country home.

two

"Rise and shine, Sleeping Beauty," a voice called up the stairs. "Rise and shine!"

Jamie groaned and turned over in her bed. "It must be the crack of dawn," she muttered, looking over at her nightstand. The brass alarm clock with its old-fashioned bells seemed to grin at her. "Eight o'clock," it rang. Hardly the crack of dawn.

"Oh, shut up," Jamie said to the clock.

She rolled out of bed and went to the window. Sun and snow dazzled her eyes for a moment. The barn across the way stood comfortably in the snow. The worn boards of the old building had long since faded to gray. Here and there a sliver of red stole some light and reflected stubborn fragments of its former glory. Jamie smiled. She remembered how years before the barn had often beckoned her to come exploring. To her surprise, today was no different. She felt drawn to it.

Jamie pulled on a pair of jeans and an evergreen sweater and ran down the stairs. She grabbed her jacket from a hook in the foyer.

"I'll be there in a minute!" she called to her grandmother.

"Jamie, breakfast is—" Kate stopped in midsentence and went to the window to watch the young woman run through the snow. "Some things never change." She smiled to herself. Memories of prebreakfast trips to the barn by a little girl in brown braids prompted the old woman to laugh. How good it was to have family in the house again!

Jamie slowed up as she approached the large doors at the front of the barn. She grasped the metal rings that served as handles and pulled open one door. The smell of hay and manure permeated the air. "I love that smell," she said aloud. "Good grief. What would Cassie say to that?" She thought of her sophisticated friend and college roommate and laughed. Cassie wouldn't be caught dead in a barn.

Despite the brightness of the morning, it was dark inside the barn. Dust danced on the fleeting shafts of light streaming through the small, grimy windows. Jamie squinted to get her bearings. A gentle lowing in one of the stalls caught her attention.

"Azalia! How are you, old girl?" Jamie scooped a handful of grain from a nearby sack and offered it to the old cow. She petted the animal's soft brown coat.

"What's new, sweetie?" she asked, gently pulling Azalia's head toward her. The cow looked at her with sad brown eyes.

"Yeah, right. What could be new around here?"

A jealous snort erupted from an elderly russet horse in the next stall.

"Merlin, I haven't forgotten you!" She rubbed the old horse's nose and hugged his neck.

Jamie looked around the rest of the barn.

"And where are your reckless cohorts this morning? Napping, I suppose, instead of hunting for mice." She searched for a sign of the barn cats, but to no avail. Then a movement from a far corner of the barn alerted the explorer to another's presence.

"What in the world?"

Jamie walked quietly over to the other side of the barn. Hidden in the shadows of an old stall stood a magnificent black horse. Even in the dimness of the stable, Jamie could see the lustre of the animal's shining coat. She stepped closer to the stall.

"Grandma didn't say anything about you," she said in amazement. Reaching over the wooden slats of the stall, Jamie put forth her hand to pet it.

Suddenly, the horse jerked away from her and snorted loudly. It angrily reared up. Jamie almost fainted with fear.

"Don't touch him!" a voice yelled at her from behind.

Someone grabbed her and pulled her away from the agitated horse. Jamie started to scream, but then she realized who had her by the arms. It was Judah.

"What the—"

"Calm down," Judah said sternly. He let go of the frightened girl and talked soothingly to the black horse. It responded to Judah immediately and whinnied softly.

"Are you crazy?" He turned to Jamie. "You could have gotten hurt." His tone softened when he saw how shaken the young woman was. "Shadow doesn't care for strangers. He's a little jumpy."

"Jumpy!" Jamie exclaimed, catching her breath. "More like crazy! I won't go near that animal again."

She looked over at the black stallion. It stood calmly surveying Jamie as if she were the animal in the stall.

"Wait a second," Jamie turned to Judah. "What is that animal doing here anyway? Grandma never said anything about a horse, and besides, she couldn't handle a thing like that." She pulled her long brown hair back with an angry motion and looked at Judah defiantly. "And what, may I ask, are you doing here?"

"So many questions." Judah walked to the horse. " 'That animal,' as you call it, happens to be mine. He's one of my hobbies." He rubbed Shadow's nose affectionately and pulled two lumps of sugar from his jacket pocket. "He loves this stuff," he said over his shoulder.

"So what is your horse doing in my grandmother's barn?" Jamie demanded, knowing she didn't want to hear the answer.

"Mrs. K lets me board him here, and in exchange I help her out around the farm. I take care of the cow and the horses and clean out the chicken coop and fix things that need fixing. My regular job is in town. I'm a mechanic." He leaned against the stall and grinned. "That answer your questions?"

Jamie looked with exasperation at the tall cowboy.

"Great," she said curtly. "Just great."

She turned in a huff and walked stiffly back to the house. She knew Judah would be following her, and she fumed.

"Of all the rotten luck. I thought I was rid of this guy, and now I find out he practically lives here."

Jamie threw open the back door of the house that opened to the kitchen. Grandma Kate greeted her with a cheery smile.

"Well, dear, I see you met up with Judah this morning. How nice! Judah, why don't you join us for breakfast?"

Jamie shot a pleading look at Kate, but Kate was oblivious to it. She set another plate on the table. Jamie and Judah sat down across from each other while Kate brought on the pancakes and sausage.

"Isn't this nice," the woman exclaimed as she busied herself around the table. "I love it when I can cook for someone besides myself!"

Judah and Jamie ate in silence. Kate brought out a book from the sideboard and opened it with loving hands.

"Today's passage is found in John 7, verses 14 to 24. Mr. King always used to say if you didn't start the morning with the Word, you'd be running on empty all day."

Jamie squirmed. Reading the Bible and praying and all that kind of thing was okay in the privacy of your home, but not in front of other people. She looked over at Judah, certain he would have a smirk on his face. To her surprise, he was leaning forward with anticipation.

"Read on, Mrs. K."

Kate read the passage. Her voice carried with it a gentleness born of love and a conviction born of faith. As she finished reading, she repeated the twenty-fourth verse.

" 'Stop judging by mere appearances, and make a right judgment.' Isn't that the truth? So many times we jump to the wrong conclusions just because of outward circumstance. It's a shame."

"It's not only a shame, but it can also be a deadly trap," said Judah seriously.

Jamie rolled her eyes. Not only was he an overgrown cowboy, but he was a fanatic to boot!

Judah and Kate didn't seem to notice Jamie's exasperation. They continued to discuss the Scripture. Jamie waited for Sunday school to end.

Finally Judah changed the subject. "Your car's running fine now Mrs. K. It was just the carburetor."

"Oh that's just fine, Judah," said Kate. She got up to clear the plates. "Now what do I owe you?"

"Nothing at all," said Judah.

"Don't be ridiculous. I'll send a check to your boss."

Judah shook his head and smiled at the old woman. "I learned a long time ago not to argue with you."

Jamie helped her grandmother clean up the kitchen. Judah, never one to sit for very long, got up and threw his jacket on.

"I'll double-check the animals. It's cold out there this morning." As he closed the door behind him, a rebel gust of cold air threatened the warmth of the country kitchen, but it was no match for the wood stove in the corner.

"We'll drop Judah off at the garage on our way to the drugstore," said Kate to her granddaughter. "Mr. Wheelock is expecting you today."

"Well, Grandma, I guess we're not wasting any time." Jamie grinned. "Don't I even get to goof off one week before I start working?"

Kate patted her on the cheek. "I didn't want you to get bored, my dear."

Bored! Jamie thought to herself. *How could I be bored in Caderville?*

"Besides," said Kate lightly as she pulled on her boots. "Your dad said you did plenty of goofing off last semester."

Jamie winced. Grandma Kate was sweet, but she was nobody's dummy. It wasn't going to be easy to have some real fun without her finding out about it.

Judah stuck his head in the door. "Car's all warmed up and ready to go."

"Just a minute," protested Jamie. "I don't even have my makeup on." She hurried up the stairs to her room and quickly applied mascara and lipstick. She pulled her hair back in a clip and glanced over at the brass clock. It seemed to say, Hurry up, hurry up.

"Oh shut up," she muttered.

She bounded down the stairs, plucked her coat from its hook, and followed Kate out the door.

"By the way, Grandma," she said as they walked to the car together. "Why didn't you tell me about that horse in the barn? It almost—"

"Oh yes, Shadow. Isn't he the sweetest animal? He's always begging for sugar and nuzzling my hand. Isn't he a beauty?"

"Yeah, right," mumbled Jamie. "That 'sweet animal' almost killed me."

"What did you say, dear?" Kate asked as they got into the car.

"Nothing," said Jamie.

Judah drove the women to the garage and let himself out.

"You drive carefully, now," he said to Kate as she took the wheel. "And nice seeing you again, Princess."

Jamie turned beet red. "The name's Jamie, if you don't mind."

The man just smiled and turned back to the garage.

"See you later," he called over his shoulder.

"Not if I can help it," Jamie said under her breath.

"Jamie! I heard that! Don't you like Judah? He's such a nice young man." Kate turned to study her grand-daughter's face.

"He's not my type," Jamie responded.

Kate said nothing more on the subject and drove to Main Street where the drugstore was located. Situated between a flower shop and a dry cleaner, it looked like something out of an old magazine. The front window

framed a small counter and soda fountain. A handful of
patrons clad in winter coats grasped coffee mugs and
nodded to one another in conversation. A bell jingled
when Kate opened the door. The gleaming wood floor
added to the old-fashioned air of the place.

A ripple of "Good morning, Kates" erupted from the
counter as the pair entered the drugstore. Kate showed off
her granddaughter before going to the back of the store.
Ben Wheelock was busy behind the divider that sepa-
rated the pharmacy from the rest of the store. Jamie could
see his gray head just over the top of the wall, customary
pen tucked behind his ear.

"Ben," Kate called to the pharmacist. "Jamie is here,
and she's raring to go."

Ben hurried out from behind the divider and took Jamie
by the hand. "Welcome back to Caderville, young lady.
Glad to hear you'd be willing to work for me. I could use
the help."

"Thanks for hiring me," Jamie responded. She had
always liked Mr. Wheelock. He had been kind to her
when she was a child, and he had a good sense of humor.

"Besides," said the gray-haired man. "I've been thinking about settling down, and there's a shortage of eligible
women around here."

"You old coot! You'd be robbing the cradle!" Kate
scolded.

"I could never compete with the loves of your life,"
interjected Jamie, in mock despair.

"Who? Who are they?" asked Ben. "Do you know
something I don't know? Who?"

"Why, the fish, of course!" Jamie grinned.

Kate let out a whoop and slapped Ben on the back.

"She's got you dead to rights, old man. You're more at home in the river than the parlor."

While they were laughing, the door to the store opened. A gust of cold air wrapped itself around Jamie's ankles and sent a shiver up her spine. The trio looked to see a blond man in a brown leather jacket walk in. Ben Wheelock stiffened.

"Mind shutting the door, Braxton," snapped the pharmacist.

"Oh yeah," said the young man. He turned back and flipped the door close. "Sorry, Wheelock." Approaching them once again, he let loose a low whistle. "And who do we have here?" he asked, eyeing Jamie.

Jamie looked into the handsome newcomer's eyes. They were steel gray. An odd feeling stirred within her. She couldn't tell if it was fear or excitement or both.

three

This guy is a knockout, Jamie thought to herself.

Kate moved instinctively closer to Jamie as if to protect her. "This is my granddaughter," she said coldly.

The threatening look in the grandmother's eyes spoke volumes to the young man. This attractive young woman was off limits.

Jamie couldn't understand why Mr. Wheelock and Grandma were acting so strange. It wasn't like either of them to behave that way. They were being downright rude!

"My name's Jamie," she said with a smile.

The young man bowed gracefully, taking her hand.

"Chad Braxton, at your service," he said. He kissed her hand.

"Who said chivalry is dead?" Jamie asked with a grin.

"Ah, fair maiden! Your sensitive heart has found me out! 'Tis but a rumor that chivalry is dead. It lives on in my heart." Chad ignored the stony looks from Kate King and the pharmacist. "Dost thou think you could join me at the Pheasant Inn for a meal this fine day?"

"Alas, I cannot join you in such sweet repast," said Jamie, striking a dramatic pose. "There are chains around my hands, my feet."

"What be those chains," Chad asked with mock concern.

"Work," she said flatly.

The two would-be actors broke into laughter. Ben and

Kate were not amused.

"Is there's something I can do for you, Braxton?" the pharmacist interjected. "If not, I have business to attend to."

Jamie swallowed her laughter. Chad shrugged his shoulders.

"I just came in for some antihistamines."

"Right this way," said Ben.

The young man made his purchase and turned to leave. "See you around, Jamie," he said with a smile.

As the door closed with a jingle, Jamie turned to Kate and her boss.

"What in the world is wrong with you two? Who is that guy, and why were you so mean to him?"

Ben took his glasses off and carefully wiped them with his handkerchief. "He's a trouble-maker, Jamie. Nothing but pure trouble."

"He's an idiot," snorted Kate.

"Grandma!" Jamie gasped. "I've never heard you call anyone an idiot before. What in the—"

"Well, there was that one time a few years ago," said Ben to Kate. "That guy that ran for mayor. You called him an idiot, as I recall."

"Oh yes," Kate mused. "I did. He lost, too, thank goodness."

"Then there was the time—"

"Will you two stop that and answer my question?" an exasperated Jamie interrupted. "Who is Chad Braxton?"

"He's the oldest son of the man who renovated the old Macintosh building. Made it into a theater." Kate put her hands on Jamie's shoulders. "Chad Braxton is a mean, disrespectful young man. He's headed for trouble and will end up nowhere. I would much rather you stayed away from him."

Jamie didn't say a word. She concluded that this Braxton guy must be a lot of fun to be around, especially if Grandma and Ben Wheelock didn't like him. They were such sticks in the mud. Perhaps this year wouldn't be so boring after all.

"Come along, Jamie." Ben changed the subject. "It's time I showed you the ropes around here. It can get pretty busy, and I want you to be ready for it."

"I'll leave you two to your work," said Kate. She kissed Jamie on the forehead. "I'll pick you up around four o'clock. Is that about the right time, Ben?"

"For today, yes. After she gets the hang of it, I'll need her until five."

"Okay. See you later!"

Jamie spent the rest of the day learning the routine of the pharmacy. She was in charge of the cash register and the soda fountain. At noon, she ate at the counter with Mr. Wheelock, but her thoughts were with Chad Braxton. She wondered if he had gone to the Pheasant Inn after all.

He certainly seems like an interesting guy, she mused. *I must tell Cassie about him. She'll be green with envy!*

The jingle of the door interrupted her thoughts.

"Hello, Princess," a deep voice sounded across the room.

Jamie scowled. "The name's Jamie, cowboy." She got up from her stool and busied herself behind the counter, determined to ignore the dark-haired man.

"All right, all right. Jamie. How's it going?" Judah asked.

"Just fine," said Jamie tersely.

"I see you two have met already," spoke Ben Wheelock. "And you really appear to have hit it off." He laughed and turned to Judah. "How did you manage to offend my employee?"

"Oh, I don't know," Judah smiled. "I guess she just doesn't like country boys."

Jamie turned around, brandishing a soup spoon. "I'll thank you both to stop talking about me behind my back," she said, her voice tinged with irritation.

"Sorry, Jamie, but we couldn't help it," replied Judah. "Now that you've turned around, though, that won't be a problem."

Ben started to laugh, but one look at Jamie's frown changed his mind. "See here, young man. Stop teasing my employee. That is my job, and my job alone. After all, I've known her since she was a little girl."

Ben smiled at Jamie. Never able to resist the old man's charm, she smiled back. "I'll go check the shelves," she said, leaving the two men at the counter.

Judah turned to Ben. "So what's new, Ben?" He lowered his voice. "I thought I saw Chad Braxton come in here this morning. Did I see right?"

Ben scowled. "Yes, it was him. Prowling around like the king of the forest."

Judah's jaw tightened. "I don't trust that guy."

"Well neither do I," replied Ben. "but it's a free country. Nothing you can do about it. He's evidently here to stay."

Judah glanced over to see where Jamie was working. She was dusting the shelves in the back of the store. Her long brown hair looked rich against the evergreen of her sweater. Her cheeks blushed with the effort of her work.

"Ahem," Ben cleared his throat to get Judah's attention. "He met her, you know. Braxton met Jamie."

Judah got up from his stool. "Maybe I better talk to her."

"Are you crazy?" Ben stopped the young man in his tracks. "Obviously Jamie is less than thrilled with you. You would only make her mad. Besides," he whispered. "Katherine said something to her already, and I think she's going to have a heart to heart with her later."

Judah nodded in agreement. "You're right as usual, Ben. I've got to get back to the garage anyway. I'll see you later."

Jamie watched Judah leave. She had seen the two men in tight conversation and had caught them looking in her direction. Resisting the urge to go over and set them straight, a determined look came over the young woman's face.

"Tonight I'll settle this Jamie-sitting-service thing once and for all, and that will be the end of it."

four

Dinner at the King house that evening was unusually quiet. Kate realized Jamie had something on her mind. After dessert, the two settled in the parlor in front of the fireplace. The yellow flames of the fire decorated the room with familiar coziness. The two women faced each other on the green sofa.

"Now, Jamie," Kate began, "I can tell you have something on your mind. I do too."

"I know, Grandma," said Jamie softly. "But do you mind if I go first? I think it would save us a lot of trouble if I told you first how I feel."

Kate nodded.

"I know you want to talk to me about Chad Braxton. I know Ben Wheelock wants to talk to me. Even that Judah guy is hovering around." Jamie took a deep breath and continued. "Do you remember when I was twelve years old and Billy Ritchfield wanted me to go for a walk with him?"

"Billy Ritchfield." Kate smiled. "I remember him. He was a little snake in the grass. I didn't trust him for one minute."

"I know," Jamie responded. "You kept quoting a Proverb, something about the 'folly of fools.' "

" 'The folly of fools yields folly.' Proverbs 14:24," quoted Kate. She laughed. "Now there's a tongue twister if I ever heard one. Try saying that one five times fast."

Jamie smiled. "Grandma! Don't try to change the

subject. Now you remember that I did as I was told—"

"Most of the time," interjected Kate.

"Grandma! Be serious." Jamie cleared her throat. "You remember that I did as I was told and did not go on that walk with Billy."

"Good thing, too! That rascal went and played around that old abandoned well at the Chambers's place. Fell and broke his leg, as I recall."

Jamie sighed. "Yes, Grandma, he did. The point is, I obeyed you." She took her grandmother's soft hand into her own. "But I was a child then. I needed you to guide me. That was fine, then. But I'm not a child anymore."

Kate's eyes misted over for a moment. "You're right, my dear. You are no longer a child. You must make your own decisions."

"Exactly," responded Jamie with relief. "I knew you would understand what I am trying to say. And I hope you will do me a favor."

"Of course, Jamie," said her grandmother.

"Please tell Mr. Wheelock and that Judah guy to back off when it comes to my personal life. They'll listen to you." Jamie got up and walked over to the mantel of the fireplace. "I don't want to hurt Mr. Wheelock's feelings. And as for Judah—" The young woman's voice became agitated.

"Yes, dear?" Kate said sweetly.

"Oh nothing. Just please do me that favor, will you?"

"Okay, Jamie, I'll tell them." responded Kate. She got up and joined her granddaughter at the mantel. Jamie's face was flushed with the heat of the fire and her eyes sparkled with the reflection of the flames. Looking into Jamie's face, Kate King realized this was no longer a twelve-year-old girl. A young woman stood before her. Perhaps this young woman still had a lot to learn about life, but it was time for her to learn it on her own.

"Jamie, I know sometimes you feel that I am preaching to you. But I want you to know I want only the best for you. I care about you."

The young woman smiled. "I know, Grandma."

"Ben cares about you, too. We all mean well," she said. "Now let me say this: I realize you think my faith in God is old-fashioned and the Bible out of date. I hope one day you discover what I did when I was young—that God is real and His Word holds the key to life."

Jamie looked away from her grandmother. She was embarrassed that Kate knew her so well.

"It's all right, dear," Kate gave Jamie a hug. "I love you no matter what."

Jamie returned her hug and sighed with relief. The Big Conversation was over. She flopped back down on the sofa.

"Now about Chad Braxton," Grandmother King spoke briskly.

"Grandma! You promised!"

"Okay, okay," Kate laughed. "I'll go make some hot chocolate."

Jamie leaned back on the sofa and stared into the fire. The illusive blues and greens melding in the flames triggered memories of other winters spent in Caderville. She could see her grandfather in his chair by the lamp, wearing his cherished brown sweater.

"Jamie girl," he used to say, "you're just like your grandma. She used to sit and stare into that fireplace for hours—"

"Hours, my foot," Kate would retort.

"For hours," Grandpa would continue. "She used to say she could see things in the fire, like princes fighting emerald dragons, all dressed in golds and blue satin." Then he would laugh with affection. "She certainly has an imagination."

"Had to have an imagination to marry you!" Kate would tease. Then the two would laugh, their laughter intertwining in the shared joy of each other's company. Even Jamie the child discerned the special love between her grandma and grandpa.

"Jamie, here's your cocoa," Kate nudged her granddaughter and brought her back to the present. "Where were you just now? Miles away?"

Jamie smiled. "Not miles. Just years."

Kate handed Jamie her a cup of cocoa. "Scalding hot, just the way you like it."

"Grandma," Jamie asked after they were both settled with their cocoa, "do you still miss Grandpa a lot?"

Kate smiled at her granddaughter. "Of course I do, dear. Your grandfather was my best friend. There are so many things I miss about him. I miss the sound of his voice. And the way he used to laugh and laugh at his own jokes, remember?" Tears formed in Kate's eyes. "I especially miss the way he used to look at me. He didn't have to say a word. His eyes were saying, I love you. Do you know, he always made me feel beautiful? Even when I turned old and gray?" She smiled and wiped her tears. "Good memories warm the heart!" she said.

A harried knock at the door momentarily startled the two women. Katherine answered the door with Jamie close behind. It was the Reverend Thomas Jacobsen.

The reverend extended his hand to Kate. "Hello, Katherine. Sorry to bother you so late in the evening," he said.

"Come right in, Thomas, and tell me what's the matter. I can tell by the tone of your voice something's wrong."

"It's Sadie Atkins. She fell down, and they're trying to convince her to go to the hospital. But you know Sadie."

Kate grabbed her coat and quickly put it on.

"Let's go. If there's anyone more stubborn and independent than Sadie, it's I."

"Thanks, Katherine," said Pastor Jacobsen. He extended his hand to Jamie. "Nice to see you again, Jamie. Sorry I don't have time to stop and visit. Hopefully I'll see you at church?"

Jamie smiled at the reverend. "Nice to see you again, Reverend Jacobsen."

"I've asked Judah to drive us," said the pastor. "That road up to the Atkins's place can be treacherous at night. He's waiting out in his truck."

Kate turned to her granddaughter. "You don't mind if I leave you here alone, do you Jamie?"

"Of course not, Grandma," Jamie replied. "You'd better hurry."

The pair rushed out the door. Jamie watched as they got into Judah's truck. She could see his outline in the cab. He honked the horn to say hello, and she reluctantly waved to him.

"Well, I shouldn't be rude, after all," she muttered.

Closing the door behind her, Jamie followed the aroma of her cocoa back into the living room. She turned on the black and white TV that stood in the corner. The reception wasn't too good, but there was nothing else to do.

"Why she doesn't buy a color TV is beyond me," Jamie said aloud. "You'd think it was a sin to watch television."

She settled for an evening game show and prepared to be bored out of her mind. During a commercial that proclaimed how natural it was to dye one's hair, the phone rang. Jamie picked up the phone in the study adjoining the living room.

"Hello?"

"Ah, fair maiden, is it really you?" a husky voice intoned.

"Chad?" Jamie asked, trying to conceal the excitement she felt.

"The very same. Chad Braxton, at your service," he said jovially. "And what are you doing this evening? Anything exciting?"

Jamie sighed. "If you call watching a game show exciting, I'm delirious with the thrill."

Chad laughed. "Actually, I don't care much for TV."

"Well, you and my grandmother have something in common," Jamie said.

"I'd have to disagree with you there," Chad spoke seriously. "I don't think your grandmother likes me at all."

The silence at Jamie's end of the line betrayed the awkwardness she felt. She didn't know what to say.

"It's okay," said Chad quickly. "I understand your grandmother. I don't mind. People like her don't see eye to eye with people like me."

Jamie felt a tinge of defensiveness rise up within her.

"What do you mean, 'people like her'?" she pointedly asked.

"Whoa, calm down. I don't mean it in a bad way," said

Chad. "Your grandmother is a devout Christian, right?"

"Yes," Jamie replied.

"Well, I'm not. I believe in doing what you feel is right for you, not what someone or some book tells you to do," Chad explained. "You know what I mean?"

"Yes," responded the young woman wholeheartedly.

"Sounds like you feel the same way," said Chad.

"Don't get me wrong," Jamie said quickly. "I respect my grandmother's beliefs. And I wouldn't let anyone bad-mouth her. But I just don't relate to her way of looking at life. That's all. We all have to make our own decisions."

"Here, here!" exclaimed Chad. "Now enough of this serious stuff. How about going to the movies with me Friday night? My Dad owns the theater so we can get in free."

"Well, I certainly wouldn't want you to spend any money on me," Jamie teased.

"Ouch, my heart," Chad cried. "You have pierced me through. Just for that, I shall have to take you out to dinner first."

"That sounds wonderful," Jamie replied. "I accept."

"I'll pick you up at seven. And it will be the Pheasant Inn, so dress accordingly."

"Okay," said Jamie. "See you tomorrow."

"Good night, fair maiden," said Chad.

"Good night, Chad," Jamie fairly whispered. She hung up the phone and hugged herself in excitement. Up the stairs she ran to get ready for bed. She donned a soft flannel nightgown and curled up on her bed. Looking at the clock, Jamie realized it was getting late. Her grandmother wasn't back yet.

What are you going to tell her? the clock's gentle ticking seemed to ask. What are you going to say about Chad Braxton?

"I'll simply tell her the truth," said Jamie aloud. "Now that we've had our heart to heart talk, it won't be hard to be open with Grandma." She stopped and sat up. "I'm talking to a clock. I must be more tired than I thought. It's time for lights out."

Jamie turned out her lamp and rested her face in the plump softness of her pillow. As she drifted off, she heard her grandmother come in the front door.

"Good night, Judah," Kate called into the night.

"Good night, Mrs. K," a strong deep voice replied.

"Good riddance," Jamie mumbled, trying to dismiss his intrusion. But the young woman fell asleep with the sound of Judah's voice resting on her mind.

five

"Jamie," Judah called to her. "Are you coming with us?"

Jamie turned to look at Judah. He was carrying a Bible the size of a refrigerator box. Kate stood next to him. She held out an iron chain to her granddaughter.

"Here, honey," she said. "This will look just lovely on you!"

Jamie dutifully lowered her head. Katherine draped the chain around Jamie's neck. It suddenly became very heavy. Jamie began to choke.

"Grandma, why are you doing this?" She tried to lift her head, but it was no use. The chain became heavier and heavier.

"It looks lovely, dear," Kate smiled.

"Help me, Grandma."

"Come along now," spoke Judah. "Time to go."

Jamie struggled again to lift her head. "Help me!" she cried out. "Help!" But Kate and Judah turned away and started down a road without her.

"Help!"

Suddenly Jamie woke up. Her sheets had become tangled around her neck. Her grandmother burst into the room.

"What in the world? Are you all right, Jamie?" Kate sat on the edge of the bed. "You were calling for help!"

Jamie pulled the sheets away and sat up. "It was just a nightmare, Grandma."

"Good grief," said Kate. "You scared me half to death."

"Me? Scare you? You were the one terrorizing me in

33

my dream!" Jamie exclaimed.

Kate let out a laugh. "That's funny! Was I chasing you with old Mr. Spoon in my hand? Remember Mr. Spoon?"

"Yes, when Mom and Uncle Frank were kids, you used to threaten to spank them with that old wooden spoon. I've heard the stories." Jamie lay back on her pillow and closed her eyes. "What time is it, anyway?"

"We might as well get up," said Kate. "It's almost seven. What time does Ben want you at the pharmacy?"

"Eight o'clock," Jamie said. Her eyes flew open. "Eight o'clock!" she exclaimed. "I've got to shower and wash my hair and blow dry it and do my makeup and eat breakfast in less than an hour!" The young woman flew out of bed and into the bathroom.

"The last time I saw you move that fast you were ten years old," Kate called after her granddaughter. "Remember? The time you threw a rock at that bees' nest?"

"Thanks for reminding me," Jamie shouted from the shower. "I can still feel those stings. And all you and Grandpa did was laugh!"

"You would have laughed too! John had to put you in the mud hole to soothe the stings. What a sight! Covered with mud except for your eyes."

"What did you say?" called Jamie.

"Nothing," replied Kate. "I'll go make breakfast."

As Jamie dressed, she thought about the nightmare. She realized how restricted her grandmother and Judah's beliefs made her feel.

"It's amazing how our dreams can express our inner feelings," Jamie said thoughtfully as she looked at herself in the mirror. "I'm glad Grandma and I had that talk last night. Hopefully things will be different now."

Jamie hurried through breakfast. Kate dropped her off at the pharmacy, promising to return at five. The day went smoothly. Jamie soon had the routine down pat. She chatted with the customers, kept track of the cash register, and served up snacks and coffee at the soda fountain.

"You're a regular pro," beamed Ben Wheelock. "Where have you been all my life?"

Jamie brushed off Ben's praise with a smile.

"It's my job," she said. "Besides, my boss is a real tyrant. I have to do well, or else!"

"Very funny, young lady," grinned Ben. "Now get back to work, or else!"

On her break, Jamie pulled on her coat and took a walk down Main Street. She found herself drawn to the old Macintosh building. It had been beautifully restored, the original carvings repaired and repainted. The marquee was tastefully designed in wood and glass, with old-fashioned letters announcing the next movie. The raised numbers 1874 on the crest of the building looked as if the years had never passed. Jamie closed her eyes for a moment and imagined it was 1874. There were horses and carriages and ladies in long dresses and street lanterns glowing in the night and—"

"Beautiful, isn't it?" observed a voice from behind.

Jamie nearly jumped out of her skin.

"Y . . . yes," she stammered.

A man with a round, kind face greeted the young woman with a smile. He stretched out his hand. "Braxton's the name. Joseph Braxton."

"Mr. Braxton," Jamie said. "You must be Chad's father."

"Guilty as charged," replied the man. "He's my oldest.

Then there's Jason, Adrian, and Luke."

"Wow!" exclaimed Jamie. "Four boys! How does your wife manage it?"

"A well-developed sense of humor," replied Mr. Braxton, "and Valium."

Jamie laughed. "My name's Jamie Carrigan. Katherine King is my grandmother. I'm spending the year with her."

"Katherine is quite a lady!" said Mr. Braxton. "She certainly can hold her own in any discussion." He rubbed his hands together. "Here we stand, in the dead of winter, shivering like a couple of kids at the pool on a windy day. Would you like to come in and see the place?" He put his key in the lock and opened the door.

"Oh, no thank you. I'd love to, but I have to get back to the pharmacy. I'm on my break," said Jamie.

"Okay, then," Mr. Braxton replied. "Don't let me keep you. Come by any time and I'll give you the grand tour!"

He disappeared into the theater, and Jamie made her way back to the pharmacy. *I'll be there Friday,* she said to herself. Jamie frowned. *I haven't told Grandma yet. She's not going to like it, but I guess she'll get used to the idea.*

Lost in her thoughts, Jamie ran right into someone.

"I'm sorry," she said, blushing with embarrassment. She looked up into the person's face. It was Judah.

"You!" she cried. "Why don't you watch where you're going?"

Judah's face suppressed a smile. "I guess I wasn't paying attention. I'll try to be more careful next time. Anyway, it's a good thing we bumped into each other."

Jamie smirked. "Yeah, right."

Judah ignored Jamie's reaction. "Your grandmother called me. She asked if I could drive you home after work. Says she's up to her elbows in apple pies. She's baking a bunch for the church bake sale Friday night." Judah looked into Jamie's eyes. "You going?"

"Home? Of course I'm going home. I'm through here at five. Try to be on time."

"No, I mean are you going to the bake sale?" asked Judah.

"Why in the world would I be going to a bake sale?" Jamie rolled her eyes. She stopped and stared at Judah. "Don't tell me you're going? You? The star mechanic and wild horse tamer? A bake sale?"

Judah looked puzzled. "Why not? I go every year. I help deliver the goods to the shut-ins."

Jamie tried not to laugh. "You're just a saint, aren't you? Underneath all that tall, dark, and ruggedly handsome exterior, you're a regular Mother Teresa."

The young man's face reddened for a moment. "You really think so?" he asked.

"What? That you're like Mother Teresa? Without a doubt—"

"No, I mean ruggedly handsome," Judah grinned.

It was Jamie's turn to blush. "I've got to go. I'll be late. Ben will throw a fit."

Hurrying away, Jamie gritted her teeth. "What did I say that for? Open mouth, insert foot. I hope he doesn't take me seriously."

Ben Wheelock was waiting at the door of the pharmacy, pencil behind ear, foot tapping the floor.

"Miss Carrigan, you are five minutes late," he said sternly. "I don't pay you to wander the streets of Caderville."

"Sorry, Mr. Wheelock," Jamie said. She hung up her

coat. "It won't happen again."

"See to it," Ben replied.

Jamie busied herself behind the cash register. The afternoon was a busy one. A steady flow of customers gave testimony that the flu season was in full swing. By the time five o'clock rolled around, Jamie was exhausted. Ben came out from behind the partition wiping his brow.

"What an afternoon, eh Jamie?" He smiled at his assistant. "Weren't bored, were you?"

"If I never see another bottle of cough syrup, I'll be happy."

The door swung open and in walked Judah. His face still sported traces of grease, and he was wearing his work overalls.

"Look what the cat dragged in," hooted Ben. "What's the matter, Judah? Fall in the tar pit?"

Judah pulled a handkerchief from one of many pockets and tried to wipe his face. He only made it worse.

Jamie hid behind her boss. "Save me, Mr. Wheelock! It's the creature from the Black Lagoon."

"Very funny." Judah stuffed his handkerchief back into a pocket. I didn't have time to change. I didn't want to be late picking you up."

"Let's leave before anyone sees us," said Jamie, half seriously.

"Kate baking pies for the sale tomorrow?" asked Ben. "I better get there early if I want to get one. They sure go fast. You're going to the sale, right, Jamie?"

The young woman was about to give a speech about everyone in Caderville expecting her at the bake sale when someone ran into the store.

"I was hoping I wouldn't miss you!" Chad Braxton

said, catching his breath. "I just got in from school. We still on for Friday night, Jamie?"

"We certainly are," Jamie said clearly. "You said seven, right?" She watched to see Ben and Judah's reaction. Ben was fuming, and Judah's black eyes smoldered. *Touché*, thought Jamie. *They got the message.*

"Yep." Chad noticed the grease-laden Judah standing next to Jamie. "My, my. Was it a bad accident? Any other survivors?"

Judah clenched his fist and took a step toward Braxton.

"Calm down, old man! It's just a joke," laughed Chad. He peered into Judah's face. "You're a mechanic down at DiLoreto's garage, aren't you? I think you worked on my BMW."

"Judah Weston." Judah held out his hand. Out of habit, Chad shook his hand, only to find his own now covered with grease.

"Wonderful," he muttered. A trace of anger flared in his eyes, but Jamie intervened.

"I better be going, now," she said hurriedly. "Grandma will be wondering where I am."

"You're right," said Judah. He held open the door for her. "Let's go."

"I'll see you tomorrow," Jamie called to Chad.

Chad watched Jamie leave with Judah.

"I'm closing up shop, Braxton." Ben pulled the shade on the front window. "If you don't mind."

Braxton left the shop in time to see Jamie get into Judah's red truck. She saw Chad through the window and wistfully waved goodbye. Judah jerked the truck into gear and pulled abruptly away from the curb. Looking into his rearview mirror, he glared at the sight of Chad standing beneath the street light, arms crossed, a confident smile on his face.

The air in the cab was thick with tension. Jamie spoke up to avoid any discussion of the young Mr. Braxton.

"It sure gets dark quick around here," she commented. The sun had already set, and the shadows of evening laced the road in front of the truck.

"Winter is kind of long here," said Judah quietly. He glanced over at Jamie, feeling suddenly idiotic about the way he looked. "Sorry I look such a mess," he said apologetically.

"Don't worry about it," Jamie responded nonchalantly. "Don't give it a second thought." *I certainly won't!* she thought.

"And listen, I'm going to talk to Grandma about driving her car to work. I can always pick her up on my break if she needs to do anything. That way you wouldn't have to bother picking me up."

"Okay."

The ride out of town to the King house was quiet from that moment on. The moon was rising, a sliver of light in the black winter sky. The edge of town gave way to country road. The hills that sheltered the valley glistened in the moonlight. Jamie loved the way the snow sparkled, as if strewn with millions of tiny jewels.

Judah turned up the King driveway and dropped Jamie off at the door. The young woman gingerly walked through the snow away from the house lights, so she could get a better look at the expanse of stars overhead.

"It still takes my breath away," she said to herself. Because Caderville was so far from any big city lights, the night sky was especially dark. The panorama of stars that glittered in that canopy of black was a wonder to Jamie. "It's as if I could see every star," she whispered.

As Judah's truck pulled out of the driveway and on to the road, he stalled it on purpose. He wanted one more look at the warm lights of the farmhouse. He needed to think about what was going on inside his head.

"Why do I get so angry lately, whenever I see Chad Braxton around?" he said to himself. "I've always known he was a jerk, but today I almost punched his lights out! Why am I so jumpy?"

He looked out toward the house. The answer to his question was standing in the field, head back, soaking in a miracle of creation. Judah hadn't expected to see her, and he sucked in his breath. He suddenly had the urge to jump out of the truck, run to Jamie, and throw his arms around her.

"I've gotta get out of here," he mumbled. "I'm going crazy." His hand was shaking as he tried to turn the key in the ignition. "Get a grip on yourself, Weston," he ordered. After what seemed like an eternity, the engine kicked in.

Judah looked up for one more view of the lone figure in the field. She was gone.

six

"What in the world were you doing, Jamie?" Kate exclaimed as Jamie came in the front door. "You'll catch your death of cold out there, and you with no boots on!"

Jamie hung her coat up and gave her grandmother a hug.

"Sorry I'm a little late," she said as she headed for the living room. Jamie sat down in front of the fire and pulled off her shoes. Her feet were cold and wet. The heat from the fire warmed away the chill.

"I suppose you were stargazing? Like mother, like daughter. Ellen used to drive me crazy, standing out there at all hours, staring at the sky. Moonstruck, starstruck, I do declare!"

Jamie slipped her feet into a pair of fleece-lined suede slippers. "What's for dinner?" she asked, heading for the kitchen. The sight of the kitchen shocked the unsuspecting granddaughter. Flour was everywhere, apple peelings draped the table and counters, and pieces of dough were strewn about.

"Don't look so alarmed, dear," spoke a frustrated Kate. "I baked six pies today. No wonder it looks like a bomb hit." She picked up an apple peel and threw it in the garbage can. "I just know I'm going to dream about apples tonight."

They cleared the table, and Kate took a pot of stew from the stove. Jamie retrieved the blue and white bowls from the cupboard.

"Those bowls have been in this house since I was a

child," said Kate. "Your great-grandmother brought them here from England. They were part of a wedding present from her mother. I still have most of the set."

Jamie had heard the story a thousand times, but she never tired of its telling. It was so romantic, the young English bride coming to America to marry her Scottish groom. Kate still had a trace of an accent now and then, especially when she was angry.

"By the way," Kate said. "You'll want to dress warmly tomorrow night. The church basement is kind of damp and drafty."

Jamie took a deep breath. "I'm not going to the bake sale. I'm going to the movies with Chad Braxton."

It was Kate's turn to be shocked.

"But I thought you'd go with me to church," she said, incredulous. "Everyone's expecting us, and it's always such a nice affair."

"It's not that I don't want to be with you, Grandma, but Chad asked me to the movies before I knew anything about a bake sale."

Katherine's lips formed a straight line at the mention of Chad Braxton. "That man is nothing but a—"

"Grandma," Jamie gently interrupted, "remember our talk last night?"

Katherine stopped and grew thoughtful. She studied Jamie's face. "Okay, you win. But I would rather you didn't develop a relationship with that Braxton. There are plenty of other young people in this town."

"Like Billy Ritchfield?"

"Billy's grown into a real nice fellow. Why, he even sings in the choir."

"Oh, brother!" Jamie sighed.

"Why don't you join the choir, dear?"

"Grandma!"

"Oh, yes, I forgot. You couldn't carry a tune in a bucket. Poor dear," Kate patted Jamie's hand and wiped an imaginary tear from her eyes.

Jamie giggled. "You are cruel, Katherine King. I'm calling the hot line. Granddaughter abuse."

They laughed together and finished their meal.

Later that night when the last light was extinguished, virtual silence filled the farmhouse. The clock on the mantel kept a solitary rhythm that dotted the air with the passage of time. The occasional creak of a floorboard and the knocking of the hot water pipes filled the darkened rooms with comforting familiarity.

In contrast to the lovely quiet was the loud cacophony of thoughts that filled the minds of the two women in the house. Each lay upon her own bed, wide awake and filled with anxious thoughts.

Jamie traced the events of the day in her mind, focusing on the troubling spots. How could she have told Judah he was handsome? It had just sort of slipped out. *I guess he is handsome, in a way,* she thought. *But he's certainly not my type. I hope he forgets I said that. All I need is him following me around!* She thought of Chad, so definitely charming and attractive. *What should I wear?* she agonized. *The Pheasant Inn is so formal. Good grief!* She sat up in bed. *What if I can't find anything to wear?* Dropping back on her pillow, Jamie recalled the scene in the drug store when Judah and Chad looked as if they were about to slug each other. And Grandma's warnings concerning a relationship with Chad. Like a runaway carousel, her thoughts went round and round, not stopping until she fell asleep, exhausted.

Kate lay awake, worrying about her granddaughter. She worried about Chad Braxton and his influence on Jamie's life. She could tell Jamie was interested in that young man. There was something about him that wasn't right. Almost as if he seemed dangerous. *Maybe I'm overreacting*, she thought. *But maybe I'm not.* Anxiety threatened to overwhelm her, but this grandmother had a weapon with which to fight. Climbing quietly out of bed, the silver-haired daughter of God got down on her knees. She took her burden to His throne and left it there. When Kate King lay her head back on the pillow, sleep came on the wings of His peace.

seven

The interior of the Pheasant Inn exuded a pleasing warmth as the handsome couple entered the foyer. Polished mahogany beams and shining brass lamps radiated elegance at every turn. A baby grand tucked in the corner sprinkled the air with music.

"No wonder people come from all over the county to dine here," whispered Jamie. "I'd forgotten how beautiful this place is."

"I do have good taste, don't I?" remarked Chad.

"And so modest, too," chided Jamie.

Chad laughed. "You certainly know how to hurt a guy."

A waiter dressed in black and white escorted the couple to a table near a window. Gazing out toward Caderville and the valley beyond, Jamie enjoyed the sleepy gleam of lights and a glimpse of borrowed silver whenever the river reflected the moon.

"Speaking of hurting a guy," Chad continued as the waiter handed them menus, "I thought your grandmother was going to kill me when I came to pick you up. If looks could kill, I'd be at the morgue even as we speak. Only I wouldn't be speaking if you get my meaning. I'd be—"

"All right already, I hear you!" Jamie sighed. "She's just set in her ways." Jamie fingered the long-stemmed glass of water the waiter had set before her. "I wish she didn't see me as a little girl."

"Well I certainly don't see a little girl sitting across from me," Chad said soberly. "I see a captivating woman.

That dress is fabulous."

Jamie tried hard not to blush. Her black off-the-shoulder silk shift was simple but elegant. She had spent an hour trying on everything in her closet before coming to a decision. From the look in Chad's eyes, Jamie knew she'd made the right choice.

"So," said Chad, "tell me about yourself."

"What an original line," Jamie smirked.

"Sorry!" Chad laughed. "So. Tell me about yourself."

"I'm from California, and I'm taking a year off from school to spend time with my grandmother."

"You mean you flunked out, got into some trouble, and your father sent you here to rehabilitate."

Jamie's mouth dropped open. She felt both anger and amazement. How in the world did he know that about her? Was it written all over her face— "delinquent drop-out?"

Chad patted her hand reassuringly. "Don't look so shocked. I'm pretty good at people analysis. And don't feel insulted. You are in the company of someone who managed to flunk out of college *twice*. I'll probably be forty-two by the time I graduate."

Jamie let out a nervous laugh. "It's nice to know we have something in common. What are you doing now?"

"I go to SUNY at Lamberton. Know where that is?"

Jamie nodded. "About ninety minutes from here, isn't it?"

"Yeah, but I only go part time. I work at a stock broker's office the rest of the time. After all," he grinned, "I have to be able to support my habits."

A tingle ran down Jamie's spine. "And what, pray tell, are your habits?"

Chad mocked a sinister grin. "Oh, evil things—fifty dollar ties, hundred dollar wine, and million dollar women, like you."

Jamie laughed. Chad Braxton was totally charming. She felt at home with him. Here was someone who understood where she was coming from and didn't condemn her! In fact, she bet he'd been through some of the things she had experienced.

While they enjoyed their meal, Jamie and Chad talked about college and shared their various escapades. Anyone observing the two young people could see they were thoroughly enjoying each other's company. Laughter periodically erupted from their table as they swapped war stories.

"And then there was the time I got arrested," drawled Chad. "TWI."

"TWI? What—"

"Talking while intoxicated."

"That's against the law?" Jamie giggled.

"It is if you're doing it in class." Chad shook his head. "My professor did not appreciate it."

Jamie frowned. "They can't arrest you for that."

"Well, I did take a swing at the guy when he insisted I leave. I felt rather insulted."

"Oh boy," said Jamie. "That brings back fond memories. My friend Rochelle and I had one too many brews and decided to referee the football game. When we refused to get off the field, they called the police. It was humiliating."

"Getting arrested is humiliating."

"No, I mean the football game. We lost 34-0. Rochelle and I were only trying to help."

They collapsed with laughter. In the midst of their revelry, Jamie pushed back the memory of the dirty jail cell. She ignored the memory of her father's face when he had come to pick her up. And most of all she shoved away the remembrance of her mother's tears in the late hours of the night. Tears for Jamie.

After dinner, Chad and Jamie hurried to the theater to catch the late showing. Mr. Braxton greeted the couple at the door.

"Miss Carrigan! How nice to see you again!" Joseph Braxton beamed. "So glad you could come this evening. I'll have to give you the grand tour—"

"Cut the hospitality speech, Dad," Chad snapped. "We'll miss the beginning of the movie."

Chad's father turned red, seething with anger and embarrassment. But he said nothing. Jamie felt embarrassed herself.

If I ever spoke like that to my Dad, he'd have my head, Jamie thought. She shot a troubled look at Chad as he stood at the concession counter. Suddenly an old conversation with her mother popped into her head.

"When you start dating, Jamie," Ellen Carrigan had said thoughtfully, "watch and see how the man treats his parents. That will be a real indicator of how he'll treat you if you ever marry him."

"Oh, Mom," Jamie had protested, "you are so old-fashioned. People don't think about things like that any more. They go by being in love. If you're in love, you marry the guy, no matter how his family life is. You're not marrying the family, are you?"

Jamie shook her head as if to shake off the memory of her mother's words. They made her feel uncomfortable.

Besides, she thought, *I just met the guy, for Pete's sake. It's not like we're engaged!*

Mr. Braxton voice broke through Jamie's thoughts. "Don't mind my son, Miss Carrigan. He's just an over-grown adolescent. He doesn't know the meaning of the word manners." He glared at his son, but Chad brushed him off.

"Lighten up, Dad."

"Enjoy the movie," the owner called after the couple. Jamie smiled and, popcorn in hand, followed Chad to the dark showing room.

The Friday night movie was the latest horror flick. Suspenseful scenes and grisly surprises pulled screams from the audience. Jamie had neglected to tell Chad that she hated horror movies. They gave her nightmares. She sat terrified and tense, which Chad thought was hilarious.

"I hate that!" she said when the heroine went down into the cellar by herself. "That is so stupid! Why do they always go down by themselves to investigate? For Pete's sake, what's she going to do when she gets there? Fight the monster with her flashlight?"

"Shh," someone hissed from behind Jamie and Chad.

"Jamie, calm down," whispered Chad, trying hard not to laugh.

"Well don't you think that's the dumbest— yep, there she goes. It's got her. She'll be dead as a doornail in a minute. Yep, there it goes. She's dead."

"Do you mind?" inquired a man seated to Jamie's right.

"Sorry," she whispered. "Look! There goes another guy. Same thing. Would you look at that?"

"Jamie, loosen up! It's just a movie!"

"Shut up. I'm scared to death."

At that Chad put his arm around her. "Poor baby," he crooned into her ear. His breath tickled her and she trembled. She didn't protest his nearness. It felt good to be close to him. All negative thoughts from the scene in the lobby disappeared.

Finally, the last victim was maimed, and the evil perpetrator was banished by the hero. Or was he? Somewhere, as usual, an odd egg lay in a corner, under a bush, portending evil and Horror Movie Part II. Jamie sighed with relief as the credits rolled and the dim lights in the theater came on.

"Are you okay?" Chad asked dramatically. "Will you need a therapist?"

"Probably," responded Jamie. "I'll have nightmares for the next two weeks."

"Oh, dear, and it's all my fault. Maybe I should stay with you tonight."

"Yeah, right." said Jamie as they reentered the lobby. "You and my grandmother can sit up all night and hold my hand."

"I forgot about your grandmother," Chad sighed. "Well, it's the thought that counts."

Chad's father weaved his way through the milling crowd and approached the young couple.

"Miss Carrigan, you look a bit green," Joseph Braxton commented. "Enjoy the movie?"

Jamie thought of Chad's arm around her. "As a matter of fact, yes."

"Next we're showing 'Driving Miss Daisy.' I think that will go easier on your stomach."

"I'm not so sure about that, Dad," Chad teased.

"Your taste in movies is abominable," responded the

elder Braxton.

"Good night, Dad," Chad said. "We've gotta go."

" 'Good night, Dad?' " Joseph gasped. "He's actually being polite! Jamie, you must be a good influence on Chad. Please, spend as much time as you can with him," he added with a grin.

Jamie straightened her back resolutely. "I shall do my best to rehabilitate the cad. I mean Chad."

"That's not fair!" protested Chad. "That's two against one."

"As I recall, those are your favorite odds," replied the father.

"Good night, Dad."

Mr. Braxton put on a serious face. "Good night, Son," he said solemnly.

Jamie laughed, and Chad threw his empty popcorn box at his father. The two threw on their coats and ventured out into the cold.

At the door of Katherine's house, Jamie and Chad stood shivering in the night air.

"I had a great time," Jamie said.

"As did I, fair maiden," spoke Chad elegantly. "I hope to make this a habit, you know."

Jamie smiled. "You and your habits! I don't know if I like the idea of being someone's habit."

"Well," said Chad diplomatically. "Why not make me one of yours?"

"I'll think about it," responded Jamie, playing hard to get.

"Now if there's anything more maddening than a woman who plays hard to get, I don't know what it is." He put his arms around Jamie. "As for playing games," he said, "I always play to win."

Somewhere in the back of her mind Chad's words disturbed her. But the little alarm that had been triggered was silenced when Chad pulled Jamie close and kissed her lightly on the lips. She was taken by surprise, not that Chad had kissed her, but that she had let him. She pulled away and looked into Chad's silver-gray eyes.

"I don't think I should . . . we should . . . uh . . ." She stumbled for words, her head spinning. "I'm not really interested in a heavy relationship, you know what I mean?"

Chad smirked and ran a hand through his blond hair. "Lighten up, Jamie. It was only a kiss!"

Jamie turned beet red. "Oh, yes. I was just kidding."

Chad pulled up the collar of his coat. "Look, I gotta go. I'll call you, okay?" He smiled and tapped her on the nose with his glove. "See you later."

Jamie watched the dark blue BMW pull out of the driveway and disappear down the road. She felt like a complete fool.

"What has gotten into me?" she said to herself. "One minute I'm melting in his arms, the next I'm babbling like an idiot." She looked up at the January moon and sighed. "I guess I'd better slow down and take it easy. Besides, you never know what a day might hold."

Jamie turned and put her hand on the brass knob of the front door. It felt cold and sent a shiver up her spine. She smiled as she closed the door behind her. "It's definitely going to be an interesting year."

eight

"The sermon this morning is entitled 'The Sparrow and the Promise.' Please open your Bibles to the Gospel of Matthew, chapter ten. We'll begin reading at verse twenty-six." Pastor Jacobsen cleared his throat and began to read: " 'So do not be afraid of them. There is nothing concealed that will not be disclosed, or hidden that will not be made known. . . . Do not be afraid of those who kill the body but cannot kill the soul. Rather, be afraid of the one who can destroy both soul and body in hell. Are not two sparrows sold for a penny? Yet not one of them will fall to the ground apart from the will of your Father. And even the very hairs of your head are all numbered. So don't be afraid; you are worth more than many sparrows.' "

Jamie looked around at the little Baptist church. The bright winter sunlight merged with the stained glass windows and passed through, scattering a riot of holy colors around the sanctuary. Reds, blues, and greens shimmered on the pews and worshippers. A rich blue-purple spilled onto the faded red carpet in a pulsing circle of tinted light. The faded brown covers of the hymn books belied the lively songs tucked between them. Jamie picked up an "I Wish" card from the holder in front of her. She scanned its contents. A check beside the appropriate square would bring about the desired result—a visit from the pastor, prayer, a favorite hymn sung. Jamie sighed.

I wish, she thought, *I were back in bed.*

Snatches of the sermon penetrated her wandering mind.

"God even knows the number of hairs on your head!" Pastor Jacobsen exclaimed. "Although, that's not such a feat in some cases, eh Clarence?"

Clarence Sunderman, the grocer, nodded his balding head. Laughter rippled through the congregation. Jamie smiled. Caderville Baptist may be boring, but it did have a sweet way about it.

Jamie returned her attention to the windows. Despite its humble size, Caderville Baptist Church had impressive stained glass windows. There were seven in all, three along each side wall and a large one above the pulpit. The wealthy logger William Cader, who made his money in the 1850s when logging on the Delaware River was a thriving business, donated the money for the windows when the original church had burned down. Kate had told Jamie the story of the original church. Rumor had it that the new young preacher, with his passionate preaching and loving manner ("Didn't hurt that he was good lookin' too," Grandpa had interjected), had stolen the heart of one of the young women in the valley. Her fiancé, a logger, hadn't taken too kindly to losing his girl, even to a man of the cloth. So one night when it was customary for the preacher to be praying in the church, a mysterious fire had been started. The wooden church had burned to the ground. Not a trace of the preacher could be found. It had been assumed he was dead until the next day when it was realized that Emily was missing too. Months later one of the faithful parishioners (they said it was Sadie Atkins's grandmother), had received a letter from some far-off place like India. The two young lovers had married and were serving together as missionaries.

It could never be proven that the logger had burned the church, but everyone knew it was he. His boss, William Cader, had somehow felt responsible and put up the money to rebuild. His crowning donation had been the windows. Each one portrayed a scene from the Gospels, with the glory of the Resurrection depicted in the soaring window over the pulpit. Jamie's favorite window was of Christ in the storm-tossed boat. His hand up-raised, he was rebuking the winds and waves. The deep blues and greens swirled around him in raging beauty, while Christ, robed in glowing white, stood like a peaceful commander, strong and in control. It was a magnificent work of art.

"That which is hidden will be revealed. Our hearts are open to Him who created us. In the hidden places of the heart we need to grow and discover the depth of God's love. Even the sparrows are watched over by the Lord. How much more does God watch over us?" The sermon was reaching its climax. "Hidden places of the heart." The words tugged at Jamie for a moment, but she shrugged them off. "Don't be afraid of those who can hurt us or even kill us. The physical realm is not the bottom line. The eternal realm is, and we can have eternal life now if we will trust in the Lord."

Jamie looked at her watch. Almost time for lunch.

"Katherine," Reverend Jacobsen called from the pulpit, "why don't you come up and lead us in singing hymn number forty-two, 'The Lord is Watching Over Me.'"

Jamie tried to look attentive since the pastor was looking in their direction. Kate got up and joined the pastor at the pulpit. As her clear voice began to sing, the congregation and pastor joined in. Jamie fumbled through the words, catching on to the chorus. "The sparrow does not fall alone, and neither then shall I; the Lord is watching over me, my hope shall never die."

As the service concluded, the pastor gave one last announcement. "Don't forget to join us today for the ice skating party. We're going up to Blueberry Lake this afternoon at two o'clock. The folks from the church at Hillside will be joining us. Hope to see you there!"

Amid the hellos and good mornings, Kate and Jamie made their way to the front doors of the church. A voice called to Jamie over the friendly hubbub.

"Jamie Carrigan!" A young man hurried over to catch her before she left. She turned to see a man in a gray suit grinning from ear to ear. "Remember me?"

For a moment Jamie drew a blank, but there was something about that mischievous grin. "Billy Ritchfield!" She held out her hand to him. "How's your leg?" she laughed.

"Very funny," Billy replied. "It's good to see you, Jamie. Are you going to go ice skating?"

She hesitated momentarily, but her grandmother jumped right in. "Of course, she's going," Kate said. "She'd love to go."

"You'll have to excuse my grandmother," Jamie spoke up in exasperation. "She still thinks I'm twelve years old."

"Mrs. King, the last time I asked Jamie to go somewhere, you wouldn't let her." Billy grinned. "Will you give me another chance?"

Kate laughed and slapped the young man on the back. "Of course, Billy." She bowed low. "You have my permission," she said formally.

"Grandma!" exclaimed Jamie. "I can speak for myself!" She turned to Billy. "I'd love to go."

"I'm just teasing, Jamie," smiled Kate. "Get cold, baby."

"You mean 'chill out,' Grandma," corrected Jamie.

"Whatever. It will be cold, by the way. Better get home and break out the long underwear!"

Jamie rolled her eyes and followed Kate out the door. "I'll see you there, Billy," Jamie called over her shoulder.

After a warm lunch and a search for the long underwear, Jamie was ready to skate. Katherine drove her granddaughter to Blueberry Lake, ten miles from Caderville. It was situated on a small, elevated plain in a cluster of hills north of the town. One side of the lake was laced with trees, and the other was dotted with summer cottages. A meadow on the eastern curve climaxed into a ridge overlooking the lake. When Jamie arrived, people were already gliding across the ice.

"I have to drive over to Lamberton and see Sadie at the hospital," Katherine reminded Jamie. "I'm not sure when I'll be back, so you'll have to get a ride home, okay?"

"No problem," replied Jamie. "Sure you don't want to stay?"

Katherine laughed. "My skating days are over. I've had my share of it though," she continued. "Your grandpa and I used to sneak up here at night when the moon was full and skate all alone, just the two of us. That was before we were married."

Jamie gasped. "Before you were married! You sneaked out of the house! And on top of that you skated, without a chaperone! Why Grandma, you wild thing you!"

"Never you mind," Katherine scolded. "Take this thermos of cocoa and have a good time. Maybe Billy can drive you home." She raised her eyebrows and smiled sweetly.

"Thanks. For the cocoa I mean, not the matchmaking advice." She leaned over and gave her grandmother a kiss. "Is anyone going with you?" Jamie asked as she got out of the car.

"I'm picking up Louise Hanson on the way."

"Good. I'll see you later!" Jamie waved goodbye and headed for the shore of the lake.

There were almost thirty people gathered for the party. Jamie scanned the crowd for Billy. She finally spotted him. He was wearing a glaringly orange parka and a purple woolen cap.

"Billy," she called. "Over here!"

Billy located Jamie's voice and hurried over to where she stood. "Glad you could make it, Jamie. It's a perfect day for skating."

Jamie had to agree. The sun was bright and the air briskly cold, but there was no wind to make it feel even colder. Jamie pulled on her skates and followed Billy to the ice.

"I must warn you that I haven't skated in a couple years," said Jamie, her ankles wobbling in the snow.

"No problem!" responded Billy. "I'm not exactly a professional myself."

"Well, at least I won't have trouble finding you in the crowd," Jamie teased.

"I know, I know," sighed the young man. "You could see me a mile away on a dark night in Transylvania. My mother bought this coat for me for Christmas. If I don't wear it at least once she'll never forgive me."

"Never mind," said Jamie. "You'll be the light of the

party!"

"Haw, haw, haw," groaned Billy. "Come on, let's skate!"

He grabbed Jamie by the hand and pulled her onto the ice. After a few faltering steps, Jamie regained her bearing and was gliding around with the best of them. She weaved in and out among the crowd. The various colored coats of the skaters created a rainbow of moving color on the sparkling ice. It was invigorating.

"Wait up," Billy called to Jamie. "I can't keep up with you."

Jamie slowed down and took his arm. "Too many lemon meringue pies?" she asked innocently.

"So I've gained a few pounds. I'm still in shape."

"In the shape of what?" Jamie laughed and skated away, with Billy in hot pursuit. She turned to look back at her pursuer and promptly forgot to watch where she was going. The inevitable occurred. Jamie bumped into someone and nearly sent him flying.

"Mr. Wheelock!" Jamie cried. "Are you all right?" She reached out her hand to steady the man.

"Jamie Carrigan, I declare, you almost knocked me into the next county," Ben Wheelock scolded. "Where in the world were you going in such a hurry?"

Billy skated to the rescue. "It's my fault, Ben. I was chasing her."

"You young people are all alike. Not a grain of sense in your heads. Why, at your age I was—"

"I know, you were done with college and working in a pharmacy," Jamie interrupted.

"I've told you that story before?" The pharmacist adjusted his cap.

Jamie nodded. "At least twice."

"Probably more like fifty times," mumbled Billy.

"What'd you say, Billy?" Ben asked.

"Pretty nifty times, back then, huh?" answered Ritchfield hastily.

"You bet. Back then, men were men, and women were women."

"You mean women were slaves," Jamie smirked.

"Oh, fiddlesticks. I'm going back to my skating. I'm pretty good, you know. Good day, and watch where you're going," Ben grinned and left the two with a semigraceful turn of the skate.

"He thinks he's God's gift to the skating world," a voice sighed behind Jamie and Billy. "But actually he's an accident waiting to happen."

"Reverend Jacobsen! Good afternoon," said Billy. Jamie smiled and shook the pastor's hand. "Last year," the pastor reminisced, "he knocked over Violet Cranberry. She fell right on her . . . ahem . . . behind. Couldn't sit in church without a pillow for weeks. I don't think she ever forgave him. No sir. When Ben Wheelock dons his skates, I stay as far away from him as possible." Jamie laughed and thanked the pastor for the information.

"Any time," Thomas replied.

"Oh, Thomas!" Ben's voice called. "I need to talk to you."

"See you later," the pastor whispered hurriedly. He dug his skate into the ice and fled from the pharmacist.

Billy shook his head and watched as Ben tried to catch up with the pastor. "Those two are a riot," he said affectionately.

Jamie studied Billy's face. "Tell me something, Billy. I never figured you to be the church-going type. Why do you go?"

The question caught the man by surprise, but he gladly answered. "I never thought I was, either. You remember how wild I was when I was a kid? Well, I was even worse as a teenager. Almost messed up my life real bad. But Pastor Jacobsen took an interest in me. And his genuine caring for a misfit like me really grabbed me. So I figured I'd try what he was preaching about. I found out it's real."

"What's real?"

"God's love," he said simply.

"Wait a minute!" hushed Jamie. "I think I hear violins! Or is it an organ?"

"Lighten up, Jamie," Billy chided. "You were the one who started this conversation."

Jamie shrugged. "You're right, I'm sorry. It's just that I hear enough of this from my grandmother. Let's change the subject."

"No problem," Billy replied. "How about we go find that thermos of cocoa? I brought some donuts to go with it."

Jamie looked puzzled. "How did you know I was going to bring cocoa?" Her eyes narrowed. "Grandma! That sneaky—"

"Jamie! Lighten up!" Billy laughed and skated back toward shore.

"I'll be there in a minute," Jamie called. "I want to skate a little more."

Almost half of the small lake was swept clean for the party. Jamie skated around the outer rim, taking in the scenery. The sky was a bright blue, a stunning contrast to the pewter hills and snow-laden fields. Here and there a bird flitted across the lake and disappeared into the trees.

Despite the talk and laughter from the party, Jamie could hear the beautiful winter stillness in the hills. She remembered the winter day her grandfather had taken her to the lake. They had climbed the ridge, and he had told her to listen.

"Listen to what, Grandpa?" ten-year-old Jamie had asked. "I don't hear anything."

"The silence, child. The winter silence. It only comes in the winter. It wraps these hills in a special quietness, like a blanket. You can almost hear the mountains dreaming, dreaming of seasons gone and the spring to come. Listen, child. You'll hear it."

Jamie smiled at the memory. How right Grandpa had been.

"Princess! Fancy meeting you here!" Judah Weston approached Jamie on his black leather skates.

"Judah! What are you doing here?" Jamie tried not to sound exasperated.

Judah looked down at his feet. "I think these are skates. I guess I'm skating."

"Marvelous."

"Seriously, I'm here with the group from Hillside Church. That's where I go to church."

"Oh," said Jamie. "Isn't that special!"

"You are the sweetest girl I've ever met!" Judah drawled. "You know how to make a guy feel real comfortable."

"Sorry," Jamie replied, "I didn't mean to. Especially in your case." She turned to head back to the shoreline.

"Nice seeing you," Judah grinned, "and don't go too near the edge over there. It might be a little thin."

"Thanks for the warning," Jamie called over her

shoulder.

She hurried away, totally aggravated. That man always made her feel like a little kid. What did he know about the ice anyway? She continued her tour of the rim and approached the edge near one of the docks. Suddenly, she heard a crack and her left foot fell as the ice broke. She let out a yell, and her other foot broke through. As the icy water hit her legs, she panicked. Abruptly the water reached her waist. She felt the bottom and tried to keep her footing. Her legs buckled beneath her.

"Help!" she screamed. "Help me!"

The next thing she knew, strong arms pulled her out and dragged her away from the hole. Jamie was weeping with fear and with relief that someone had rescued her. Judah Weston ripped off his coat and wrapped her in it. By then, several people had hurried over, among them Billy Ritchfield.

"What happened?"

"She went too close to the dock." Judah snapped. "Give me your coat."

Billy quickly unzipped his down coat and threw it over Jamie. "I'll get Ben."

"Put me down," Jamie recovered herself. "I am fine. You're embarrassing me."

Judah ignored her and carried her toward the cars. Ben and Thomas signalled Judah to bring her over to their cars.

"My car heats up fast," yelled Ben. "Put her in here. Thomas is going for the doctor. We've got to get her home immediately."

Jamie protested, but she was shivering uncontrollably. Judah tightened his grip on her and headed for Ben's car.

She was about to say something sarcastic, but the look on Judah's face stopped her short. He looked frightened and concerned, as if he knew it could have been much worse. She could have slipped beneath the ice and—

At the thought of such a horror, Jamie passed out in Judah's arms.

nine

When Kate King pulled into her driveway, she saw Judah's truck and four other vehicles parked in front of the house. She recognized the doctor's car. He rarely made social calls. Her heart started to pound.

"Jamie!"

She jumped out of her car and ran to the front door. Ben opened the door and tried to reassure her.

"She's all right, Kate," he said firmly.

Kate ignored him and started for the stairs. She didn't see Judah and Billy holding blankets in front of the fireplace.

"Bring up one of those blankets and be quick about it!" the doctor commanded from upstairs.

Kate rushed into Jamie's bedroom. The doctor was bending over her, taking her pulse.

"Grandma!" Jamie said. She tried to sit up but the doctor promptly forbade her to do so. He turned to look at Kate and frowned.

"I don't need you fluttering around in here. Go back downstairs," he growled.

"I will not," Kate retorted. She took Jamie by the hand and kissed her on the forehead. "What happened?"

"She fell through the ice," Judah replied as he walked in the room. He handed the doctor a blanket. The physician removed the blanket on Jamie and covered her with the newly warmed one.

"It was all my fault," Billy said woefully, following

Judah into the room. "If only I hadn't left her alone. But I went to get the cocoa and the donuts and then I heard a commotion and—"

" 'If only I hadn't left her alone,' " Jamie mimicked Billy with a whine. "For Pete's sake, I'm not a child! So the ice broke, big deal! If you had been with me, the whole lake would have caved in and then we'd all be under the care of this charming doctor."

"That's not funny!" protested Billy. "I'm not that heavy, and besides, you shouldn't be—"

"What in the blazes is everyone doing in this room?" barked the doctor. "Everybody out or I'll throw you out." He nodded at Kate. "Go see what the devil's taking so long for Ben to make that hot water and whiskey."

The three visitors walked obediently out of Jamie's room and down the stairs. In the kitchen Ben was sputtering over the stove. The tea kettle finally began to whistle.

"It's about time," the pharmacist grunted. He took the bottle of whiskey on the table and poured some into the cup. Then he added a dollop of sugar.

"Doc Stanton wants that right away," said Kate.

"I would have had it right away if you didn't keep your whiskey in some forgotten corner of your cupboards. I found it behind a fossilized jar of honey."

Kate reached for the cup, but Ben refused.

"I'm taking it up," he said. "I need to talk to Stanton about medication for her in case she gets sick."

Kate sat down wearily at the table. Judah joined her while Billy warmed another blanket. Cupping his hand over hers, Judah smiled at the shaken woman.

"She'll be fine," he said.

"I know," responded Kate. "It's just such a frightful

thing. Who pulled her out?"

"I did," said Judah. His black eyes narrowed for a moment. "I shouldn't have let her go near the docks."

"You heard her, Judah," Kate reminded the young man. "She's got a mind of her own. I just hope this is the worst trouble she gets into."

Judah nodded and his jaw tightened. He thought of Chad Braxton and his smooth ways. How he wished Braxton had never showed his face in Caderville. If he ever caught that creep doing anything underhanded to Jamie he'd—his hands clenched.

"Judah!" Kate intervened. "Calm down." She studied his face. "I know what you're thinking. You're just going to have to trust the Lord to watch over her. He was watching over Jamie today. You were there to pull her out and bring her home safely. I pray for her every day. And today you were part of an answer to my prayer. Thank you."

She smiled. Judah blushed and ran a hand through his tousled black hair. "Where's that other blanket!" came a familiar shout from upstairs.

Billy Ritchfield ran up the stairs and back down again. He joined Judah and Kate in the kitchen.

"That man has the disposition of a camel!" he whispered.

Kate laughed. "Yes, but he's saved more lives in this county than any other doctor I've known. He can read a situation like a book and solve it in a matter of minutes. It's something to see."

"Well, he could at least be civil," Billy complained. "I hate getting yelled at. It makes me feel like a kid."

"Buck up, soldier," Judah slapped Billy on the back.

The night is young."

Kate got up to look out the window over the sink. The sun had already gone down. She reached over and turned on the back light. Shadows from the house stretched to join the darkness in the outer edges of the yard. The dim shape of the darkened barn brooded in the background. It was going to be a long night. Before going back upstairs, she whispered a prayer of thanks that Jamie was all right.

"She wasn't in the water long enough to warrant taking her to the hospital," Dr. Stanton explained. "However, she was in long enough to get chilled to the bone."

"You can say that again," said Jamie. "Can I have some more of that hot toddy stuff?"

The doctor nodded, and Ben left to make more of the hot drink for the patient.

"As I was saying," the doctor continued, "she was in long enough to get chilled to the bone. She'll be fine, but in all likelihood she will probably come down with a sore throat and fever, then a full blown case of the flu. What is your history with fevers, young lady?"

"Oh, we go way back," replied Jamie with a grin.

"She has a tendency to get high fevers," interjected Kate. "At least she did when she was a child."

"That doesn't help me now," the doctor said brusquely. "What about as an adult?"

"Still high," said Jamie. She frowned at the thought of it. "The last time I was sick, my fever was so high I—" She shivered. "It was awful."

"Then you can expect the same," said the doctor. "Just give her extra-strength acetaminophen every four hours and keep cool compresses on her head. That should help. I've given Ben a prescription for an antibiotic. Just follow the directions. She'll be fine."

He picked up his bag and headed down the stairs. Kate walked him to the door.

"Thanks for coming, Doctor," she said.

He grunted and put on his coat and hat. "You know I don't often make house calls. But Wheelock wouldn't take no for an answer. Make sure the girl doesn't do something foolish like galavanting out of bed too soon. I don't want to medicate her now in case she gets by without getting sick. That's not likely, though. She'll probably get ill, but she'll be okay. Call me if you have any doubts about the situation."

Giving Kate a mere hint of a smile, he was gone.

"Grandma!" Jamie called. "Get these people out of here!"

Kate smiled and shooed the men out of Jamie's room. She adjusted Jamie's pillows and checked her blankets.

"How do you feel?"

"I feel fine, Mommy. Now where is my teddy bear?" Jamie sighed. "Grandma, you don't need to fuss over me. That hot toddy really warmed me up. I'm just tired now, that's all."

"Okay, dear, you go to sleep. I'll send everyone home," said Kate. She turned off the light on Jamie's bedstand. "I'll leave the hall light on."

"Good," said Jamie. "I wouldn't want the bogyman to get me!"

"Stop being silly! I'll get that old bell we used to use whenever Ellen or Frank was ill. You can ring that if you need me."

Down in the kitchen, Kate tried to persuade Judah, Billy, and Ben to go home.

"She's going to sleep now," she said. "It's not necessary for you to stay any longer."

"If you're sure you don't need us," said Judah.

"We're not in any hurry," Billy volunteered.

Kate smiled. "We'll be fine."

The two young men reluctantly put on their coats.

"I'll be back tomorrow," said Judah.

"Yes, we'll be back tomorrow," agreed Billy, shutting the door behind them.

Ben stood his ground. "I'm going to run over to the store and fill this prescription. I'll pick up some liquid acetaminophen too." He put on his coat. "Be back in a few minutes. I'll be sleeping on the couch."

"Ben Wheelock!" Kate exclaimed. "I really don't think that's necessary. I appreciate your kindness, but I can't expect you to stay here tonight."

"I'm staying," he said matter-of-factly. "You may need me."

Kate threw her hands into the air. "Can't talk sense to you when you're like that," she sighed. "I'll fix the couch for you. Just let yourself in. I'm going to check on Jamie and go to bed."

Jamie was sound asleep. Kate placed her hand on the young woman's forehead. It felt normal.

"Sweet dreams, and the Lord bless you," she whispered. Then she got ready for bed herself.

Ben returned from his mission and called quietly up the stairs to Kate. "I'm here now," he said. "Good night."

"Good night," Kate whispered loudly from the top of the stairs.

Jamie woke up to see a tall man in a large orange parka standing next to her bed.

"Who are you?" she whispered, her heart pounding.

"The bogyman," he said calmly.

"Oh," Jamie turned on to her side. "Good night."

Suddenly her eyes flew open. The bogyman! What? She turned around and he was gone. Billy Ritchfield was sitting on a bench eating lemon meringue pie.

"Billy, what are you doing here? It's late, and I'm trying to sleep!"

Billy just ignored her and continued eating.

Violet Cranberry came out from behind Billy and offered Jamie a pillow. "Here, dear, you'll feel better." She put the pillow over Jamie's face.

"I can't breathe!" Jamie cried. "Get it off me!"

She struggled for a moment and finally climbed out of bed. The floor felt cold to her feet. "Wait a minute," Jamie panted. "This isn't my floor! This is ice!"

She slipped and fell. The ice cracked, and Jamie felt herself falling and falling into hot water. It was so hot.

"Help," she cried. "I'm drowning!"

Judah pulled her out and placed her back in bed. He started piling blankets on her. It was so hot.

"No more blankets," Jamie muttered. "Too hot."

"Doctor's orders," said Dr. Stanton. "Here, put this on." He handed her the orange parka.

"Want a donut?" asked Billy.

"Help!" cried Jamie, gasping for air. "It's too hot. I can't breathe. Somebody help me!" She reached over to ring the bell, but she dropped it. Jamie watched it fall into a large hole in the ice. "Help!"

Her cries for help jerked Kate awake. She ran into Jamie's room. Her granddaughter was writhing on the bed, moaning. Kate touched Jamie's forehead.

"She's burning up! Ben! Get up here!"

Ben bounded up the stairs, medicine in hand.

"Try to hold her still, and I'll get this stuff down her," he ordered.

Kate put her hands on Jamie's shoulders and spoke soothingly to her. "It's okay, honey. I'm right here. It's okay." Jamie responded long enough for Ben to administer the medicine.

"Ben, you stay here while I get a washcloth," Kate instructed. She ran to the bathroom, grabbed a cloth, and stuck it under cool water. She hurried back to the room and placed it on Jamie's feverish head.

"Too hot," the young woman mumbled. "Too many blankets. Watch out for the ice," she warned.

"It's okay, Jamie. You're going to be fine." Kate turned to Ben. "There's a basin under the bathroom sink. Fill it with—"

Ben was out of the room before she could finish. He returned with lukewarm water and extra washcloths.

"We've got to be careful not to give her a chill," he said. "Keep up the washcloths until the medicine kicks in. Then she should be better."

Kate smiled and handed the pharmacist the washcloth. "Thanks for staying, Ben."

He wrung out a fresh cloth and gave it Kate.

"I told you so," he said.

Ben sat down in a chair with the basin on his lap. They continued the washcloth treatment. Jamie tossed and turned, moaning with fever. Finally, the young woman quieted down and fell into a deep sleep.

The next morning, Jamie awoke with a sore throat and the aches and pains of flu. She felt like she'd been through a war.

"Oh, my aching head," she muttered. She tried to sit up but found herself too weak and dizzy.

Kate bustled into the room.

"Good morning, dear," she said, checking Jamie's forehead for fever.

"What's so good about it?"

"You had quite a night," her grandmother said softly. "Scared me half to death!"

Jamie frowned. "Did I act strangely?"

"Well, you were hallucinating because of the fever. That's all. You kept talking about the ice and the blankets."

"Oh no. I was afraid of that. I remember something about the bogyman and Billy. It's vague to me. I hate that!"

"You mean to tell me that's what happens when you get a fever? Why didn't you tell me?" Kate shook her head. "At least I would have been prepared!"

Jamie sighed and closed her eyes. "I didn't want to worry you. And I was hoping it wouldn't happen, anyway."

"It's over now. Can I bring you something to eat?"

"No, just something to drink. My throat is killing me."

Ben knocked on the open door. "May I come in?" he asked. "It's time for your medicine."

"Mr. Wheelock!" the patient exclaimed. "What are you doing here?"

"It's a long story," he replied, handing her three pills. "Antibiotic and something for your headache and sore throat pain."

"How did you know I—? I give up."

Kate helped Jamie with the medication. After taking a drink of cool water, Jamie put her head back on the pillow.

"How's the fever? Gone?" asked Ben.

"Yes, thank goodness," responded Kate.

"Judah and Billy are here," Ben said. "They wanted to see how you were doing."

There was no response.

"She's asleep, Ben," whispered Kate. "Let's go."

Down in the kitchen, Judah and Billy sat at the table talking quietly.

"This isn't a funeral home," laughed Kate as she entered the kitchen. "You don't have to whisper!"

"We didn't want to disturb Jamie, Mrs. King," said Billy.

"How is she?" asked Judah, his voice reflecting the concern he felt.

"She's sick, just like the doc said she'd be," Ben replied.

"Yes, but it's flu, not the plague, so everybody cheer up, for heaven's sake," exhorted Kate. "Now who wants pancakes?"

"No, Katherine, you are not cooking for us this morning," Ben spoke firmly. "You had a rough night. You need to rest yourself. We were just leaving, right, men?"

Judah and Billy hastily agreed and headed for the door.

"If you need anything, just give me a buzz," said Ben as he pulled on his coat. "Tell Jamie not to worry about work this week. I can handle it until she gets better."

"Thank you, Ben." Kate smiled at her old friend. "Thanks again for helping us out."

Billy pulled open the door, and there stood the pastor,

his hand raised, ready to knock.

"Good morning, Reverend Jacobsen," Billy greeted him.

"Good morning, Billy. I've come to see how the young lady is doing." He looked around at the men in the foyer. "Apparently so has the rest of Caderville."

"Come on in," said Kate. "They were all just leaving."

The three men left, and Kate escorted the pastor into the parlor.

"I'm sorry I've come so early this morning, but I was concerned. How is Jamie?"

"She's not feeling well, but she'll be fine. She's come down with the flu."

"I'm glad to hear it worked out all right. She gave us quite a scare. I was afraid she'd end up with pneumonia or something."

"No, thank the Lord. It was like you described in your sermon yesterday. The Lord certainly was watching over Jamie at the lake. I want to share it with Jamie."

The pastor gently took Kate's hand. "Be careful what you say, Kate," he said hesitantly. "Now don't take offense, but I don't think she's quite ready to hear it. If we overstep our bounds, it might push her farther away. We each have to find our own way."

"You are a wise man, Reverend Jacobsen," Kate replied. "I know I can be kind of pushy sometimes. Jamie already talked to me about my preaching."

"Good! I'm glad you two can talk! You tell her I was here and that we're praying for her." The pastor stood up. "You look like you could use some rest yourself, Mrs. King. I'll let myself out."

Kate thanked him and sighed with relief after he was

gone. She appreciated everyone's concern, but right now all she wanted to do was sleep. The weary grandmother closed her eyes and fell asleep on the green sofa. The old farmhouse sheltered the two exhausted women, and the trouble of the night before dissolved in deep sleep.

ten

"You can't use that! Since when is 'en' a word?" Jamie said accusingly.

"It's right here," replied her grandmother. "Mr. Webster will prove me right." She proceeded to read the definition. " 'An en is half the space of an em.' It's right here. Want to read it?"

"Never mind," said Jamie. "Now you're out, and you get four points for it. You win again."

"Better luck next time," Kate said.

"What next time? You always beat me at Scrabble. I only won once, and I think you let me win that time."

"Well, I didn't want you to get discouraged."

"Thanks." Jamie pushed back her covers. "I feel much better. It's been three days. I'm going to get dressed."

"All right, Jamie. I'll fix lunch."

Jamie felt a little weak-kneed as she climbed down the stairs. She settled herself in the living room. The phone rang, and Kate answered it.

"It's for you," she called to Jamie. Jamie could tell by the tone of her grandmother's voice that she wasn't too pleased with the caller. Jamie picked up the phone in the study.

"Hi Chad!" she with a smile in her voice. She heard the click of the kitchen phone as Kate hung up.

"How'd you know it was me?" Chad's voice was a welcome sound to Jamie's ears.

"Never mind how I knew. What's new?"

"What's new? There's been talk all over town about the young woman from California who fell through the ice and barely escaped with her life." Chad sighed. "I turn my back on you for one moment, and you try to kill yourself. Really, Jamie, I didn't know you cared!"

Jamie laughed. "You are so vain! I thought you'd be in school today. What's up?"

"They canceled classes this afternoon. So here I am, at home with nothing to do."

"Why don't you come over?"

"Do you think your grandmother would let me in?" asked Chad.

"Of course she will!" said Jamie. "Don't worry about Grandma. Besides, I am bored out of my mind and suffering from a severe case of cabin fever. Maybe you could cheer me up."

"I shall do my best, fair maiden. I'll be over at two o'clock."

Jamie hung up and hugged herself. Chad Braxton was coming! Whenever she thought of him, her heart fairly skipped a beat.

"Those eyes of his! He is so gorgeous," she said to herself. "Jamie, get a grip on yourself. Looks aren't everything." She paused for a moment. "Looks!" she shrieked. "What about me? I'm a total wreck! I must look like something the cat dragged in."

"You don't look that bad," Kate said. She put a tray in front of her granddaughter. "Cold chicken and mayonnaise, just the way you like it."

"Thanks," Jamie said. "Chad's coming over this afternoon. I hope you don't mind." She braced herself for an argument.

"That's fine, dear. I've got a lot to do this afternoon. I'll stay out of your way." Kate ignored the shocked look on her granddaughter's face. "Besides, it will be nice for you to have some company."

Kate left the room humming a tune. Jamie finished her lunch, trying to digest her grandmother's behavior. Her grandmother had acted a little different all week. Jamie had waited for a sermon about God watching over the sparrows, and how He had watched over Jamie that Sunday. But the sermon had never been delivered, and now Kate was not even protesting Chad Braxton's visit. For a moment, Jamie felt a little disappointed and perhaps unsure of herself. She shrugged off her feelings and climbed the stairs to get ready for Chad. At two o'clock, the blue BMW pulled into the driveway. Jamie let Chad in and showed him to the living room. He looked around the room and through the door.

"Where's your grandmother?" he whispered.

"She's upstairs working on something," Jamie whispered back. "And you don't have to whisper," she laughed aloud.

"What's she doing? Polishing her shotgun?"

"Stop it! She's not that bad," Jamie smiled.

Chad sat down on a rocking chair and looked Jamie over.

"You look a little pale, Jamie," he said with concern. "Maybe I shouldn't have come."

Jamie shook her head. "I'm glad you came. I've got a bad case of cabin fever, but I'm not quite strong enough to hit the road."

Chad leaned forward in the chair. "What can I do to entertain you?" he asked.

The sincerity in Chad's gray eyes touched Jamie's heart. He made her feel special. The young woman's heart stirred with feelings she struggled to ignore.

"Aha!" Chad exclaimed, his eyes catching sight of the Scrabble box. "I haven't played this in years! When I was at Penn State, I was the champ of my dormitory."

He picked up the game and set it up on the coffee table.

"Wonderful," Jamie muttered. "Now I can be soundly beaten by someone other than Grandma."

"Chin up, old girl. Let me dazzle you with my fabulous vocabulary!"

Jamie put up a good fight, but when Chad managed to use all his letters by spelling out "quicken" on a triple word space, she gave up.

"Let's see," figured Chad, engrossed in totalling up his score. "Well, the Q is on a double letter space, so that's twenty; hmm, all together that's thirty-two points. And it's on a triple word space, so that's three times thirty-two. Now what's that?"

"Ninety-six, to be exact," replied a disgusted Jamie.

"Oh, yes, I almost forgot! I get fifty points for playing all my letters! Isn't that wild?"

"Wild. Really wild. You just made one hundred and forty-six points with one play. Can we quit now?"

"How about a coffee break?" Kate walked in with a tray laden with pie and cookies.

"Wow! That smell great!" said Chad. "Good afternoon, Mrs. King."

"Hello, Chad," said Kate. "Would you two like coffee or cocoa?" Emptying the tray's contents on the other end of the coffee table, she glanced at the game. "Whoa! Who made 'quicken'? That's a whopper!"

Jamie flopped back on the couch. "Take a wild guess!"

"Well, it couldn't be you. Must have been Chad."

Chad laughed. "Sounds like you have quite a Scrabble reputation, Jamie."

"Yeah," replied Jamie, "a bad one."

A knock at the back door in the kitchen called Kate away from the postgame analysis.

"Hello, Judah," Jamie heard her grandmother say in the kitchen. "Come on in."

"I can't stay," Judah said. "I'm on my break. I just stopped by for a minute to see how Jamie is doing."

"Come and see for yourself!" said Kate.

"Oh, no, Mrs. K. I'm a mess, I mean I came straight from work, you know, and . . ." He looked down at his grease-stained overalls.

"Who cares? Come on in to the living room." She looked him over. "Just don't sit down or touch anything," she said with a laugh.

Judah reluctantly followed his hostess to the parlor. He knew what to expect. He had seen the BMW in the driveway. He braced himself to be polite to Chad Braxton.

"Hello, Jamie," Judah greeted the young woman. "Braxton."

"Hello, Judah," Jamie said. She had not seen the tall, dark man since he had pulled her from the lake. Somehow, Jamie didn't feel quite so aggravated to see him as she had thought she would be.

"Sorry to interrupt. I just wanted to see—"

"I'm just fine," the young woman replied. "I'll be back to work on Monday."

"You sure you'll be ready?" asked Judah. "You don't want to overdo it."

Jamie smiled and shook her head. "I'll be fine. Thanks for asking."

The gentleness in her voice made Judah's heart pound. Jamie surprised herself with the way she was talking.

"Ever play Scrabble, Weston?" Chad's voice snapped through the air.

Jamie was startled by Chad's tone. Judah merely ignored it.

"No, as a matter of fact I don't," said Judah.

"Oh, that's right. I guess the vocabulary of a mechanic wouldn't cut it, would it?" sneered Chad.

"You're rather an imperious fellow, aren't you Braxton?" Judah replied smoothly.

"Touché!" said Kate under her breath.

"I've got to get back to work," Judah said. "I'm glad you're feeling better, Jamie."

"I'll walk you out," Kate volunteered hastily.

After Judah left, Jamie turned to Chad with a questioning look. "What was that all about?" she demanded.

"What?" asked Chad innocently.

" 'Do you play Scrabble, Judah?' Mechanic's vocabulary? Why were you baiting him?" She stared at him in amazement.

"Oh, that! I just like to rile the guy, that's all. He is such an uptight dude," Chad said. "Besides, maybe I should ask you the same question."

"What?"

"What was that all about? Your sweet alluring voice when you spoke to that idiot," challenged Chad. "Do you have a crush on him?"

Jamie turned bright red. "You're crazy, Chad Braxton!" She threw a pillow at him. Then she stopped short of throwing another one.

"Wait a second," she said accusingly. "Do I detect a hint of jealousy here?"

Chad bit his lip. "Ouch," he said. "You weren't supposed to notice." He sat down next to Jamie on the sofa. "I know he saved you from the evil clutches of Blueberry Swamp, but that doesn't mean you have to fall for the guy." He moved closer to her. "After all, I'm better looking, more suave, and a lot more fun, don't you think?"

He gazed intently into Jamie's eyes with a look of sincere desire. Jamie swallowed hard. He was so hard to resist. She took in his perfect hair, his perfect eyes, his perfect lips. Chad seized the moment and leaned over to kiss her. Jamie closed her eyes in anticipation.

Smash! Clatter! Clang! The kiss never came. Kate dropped the large metal serving tray just outside the parlor door. Chad nearly jumped out of his skin.

"Oops!" Katherine apologized. "Dropped my teeth!"

She picked up the tray and walked through the living-room doorway, laughing. "That's what my father used to say if anyone dropped something that made a huge noise: 'Did you drop your teeth?' He was a jokester, my father."

"I thought it was a shotgun," Chad blurted out, with an emphasis on the word shotgun.

"Silly boy!" Kate busied herself with cups and plates.

Jamie suddenly felt very tired. *I don't believe this is happening*, she thought.

"I'll take that," Chad said. He picked up the tray to carry it to the kitchen. "I better be going now, anyway. You look tired, Jamie."

Jamie nodded and let out a long sigh. "You're right. All

this excitement has drained my energy."

"Don't get up," smiled Chad. "Your grandmother will see me out, I'm sure."

Jamie laughed. "Thanks for coming, Chad."

"My pleasure," he said aloud. "Almost," he whispered.

"Stop!" Jamie hushed him. "She's not deaf, you know."

He grinned, balanced the tray on one hand, and tipped an imaginary hat.

"Don't drop that tray!" Kate called from the kitchen.

"I'm coming," responded Chad. He winked at Jamie and left her alone in the parlor with her thoughts.

When she heard his car start up, Jamie lay down and closed her eyes. The last thing she heard before she fell asleep was her grandmother in the kitchen whistling "Onward, Christian Soldiers."

eleven

"Jamie! Your dad's on the phone!" Kate called upstairs to her granddaughter.

Jamie went into her grandmother's room and picked up the extension. "I've got it, Grandma," she said into the receiver.

"Dad?"

"Jamie girl! How are you? Been ice skating lately?" Her father's deep laugh filled Jamie's ear.

"Very funny, Dad," Jamie said. "That was two months ago."

"So how's everything?"

"Fine. I work, I eat, I sleep. I play Scrabble."

"No excitement?"

"Well, not really," Jamie hesitated. What was he driving at?

"Your grandmother tells us there's a new man in your life!" Her father's voice sounded ever so slightly agitated.

Jamie let go an audible sigh. "You mean Chad?"

"That's the one. Chad Braxton, I believe?"

"What about him?"

"Kate doesn't seem to like him very much, Jamie girl. And that must mean he's like one of the good-for-nothing jerks you hung around with at college." His voice tightened with displeasure. "Who is he?"

"Dad," Jamie began, her blood beginning to boil, "his father owns the theater, he's a senior at SUNY Lamberton, it happens to be none of your business, and I would hang up on you but you're my father!"

There was silence on the other end of the line. Jamie's father cleared his throat. Jamie could hear her mother's frustrated "Dan!" in the background.

"I'm sorry, Jamie. I didn't intend to call and interfere. You know I care about you, and I worry about who you spend your time with. You know what your mother always says—"

" 'He who walks with the wise grows wise, but a companion of fools suffers harm.' Proverbs 13:20," Jamie quoted in a sing-song voice. "She made me memorize it when I was a kid. Give me a break. Dad, I'm twenty-two, remember? When are you going to accept the fact that I am not your little girl anymore?"

"Okay, okay, let's not get started again on the 'I'm not a child anymore' argument. We've been over that enough as it is. But as for it being none of my business, you will always be my business, even when you're fifty-two." He paused a moment. "Let's make a deal. I'll let you know what I think, but I won't tell you what to do, how's that?"

"Deal," responded Jamie. "Now, how's Mom?"

"She's uh, fine."

Jamie noticed a slight change in her father's voice. "What's the matter, Dad? Is she all right?"

"Yes, she's fine," he said quickly, handing his wife the phone.

"Hi honey, how's it going?" Ellen Carrigan's voice was strained.

"What's the matter, Mom? You sound funny. What's going on?"

Jamie's mother ignored the question. "We've got a

surprise for you. We're flying out for Easter."

"Great!" Jamie exclaimed. As much as she was glad to be away from home, she did miss her parents. "That's only a few weeks away."

"I've got another surprise as well," said Ellen. "Your friend from college wants to come and spend a few weeks with you this summer."

"You mean Cassie? Fantastic!" Jamie fairly shrieked.

"We'll talk about it at Easter. I don't want Grandma to get worn out."

"Grandma won't mind! You know, the more the merrier. It'll be great!"

"We'll discuss it then. Take care of yourself. Now let me talk to Grandma."

Jamie called down to Kate, and then she hung up the phone. She went back to her own room and flopped onto her bed. In her excitement about seeing everyone, she had forgotten to pursue the subject of her mother. Why did she sound so strange? And what was up with Dad? Jamie felt a knot form in her stomach.

"I don't know," she thought aloud. "I've got a bad feeling that something's really wrong. What could it possibly be?"

"Jamie, can you come here?" Kate called up the stairs.

"Coming!" Jamie answered. She bounded down the stairs and into the kitchen. "What's up?"

Katherine stood over the stove, stirring up something in an old iron pot.

"Take this out to Merlin, would you?" she asked. She poured the contents of the pot into a large dog-food bowl.

"What king of concoction is that?" Jamie asked, wrinkling her nose.

"It's a special mush for Merlin. I think he's feeling a bit poorly today. Your grandfather used to make this for the animals whenever they took sick. It works wonders."

"Wonder Mush. Why don't you market it?" Jamie laughed over her shoulder. She got her coat and pulled it on.

Kate handed her the bowl. "Here. Nurse for a day."

Jamie took the bowl and hesitated. "Grandma, did you notice anything strange today about Mom and Dad?"

A serious look flitted across Kate's face and was gone. "No, I don't think there was anything really—"

"Grandma!" demanded Jamie. "I can tell when you're avoiding an issue. What's going on?"

Kate patted Jamie's cheek. "Nothing your Mom and Dad can't handle," she said. But her eyebrows knit together betrayed the concern she felt in her heart.

Jamie braved the cold March wind and pulled open the barn door. Azalia and Merlin both turned their heads to see who was their latest visitor. The annoyed look on their faces said, "shut the door and be quick about it."

"You old dears," Jamie murmured sweetly to the pair of animals. "Look Merlin, I've got just what the doctor ordered: Wonder Mush."

She stuck the bowl in front of the elderly horse. He nodded his thanks and began to eat, with a jealous Azalia looking on.

"Good morning, Jamie," a voice spoke from the back of the barn.

"Judah!" Jamie sucked in her breath. "Why do you insist on sneaking around and scaring me half to death all the time?"

"If you call parking a fire-engine-red truck in plain view of the house sneaking around, I guess I'm guilty.

Sorry I startled you. Again."

"It's okay," Jamie said. She peered over into the corner of the barn. "How's your wild horse doing?"

Judah came out from among the shadows and smiled at Jamie. "He's not wild, honest. Come here and feed him some sugar."

Jamie hesitated. "I'd rather keep my distance."

"Come on," Judah insisted. "Come here."

The young woman walked slowly toward the back of the barn.

"Hold out your hand," Judah said.

Jamie held out her hand, and Judah placed two lumps of sugar on her palm. Speaking softly to the stallion, Judah cupped his own hand beneath Jamie's and guided it close to the horse's mouth. Shadow eyed Jamie for a moment and then took the sugar.

"See, he's not wild. He just needs to get to know you. Let's try it again."

Out came more sugar, and Judah cradled Jamie's hand in his own. Jamie thought she felt his hand tremble for a moment. She studied his face. He didn't look at her but concentrated on the horse. *I wonder what you're thinking right now,* the young woman thought. At his touch, Jamie herself felt something faintly stir in her heart. *No way,* she thought.

"Mother Teresa," she said aloud, trying to snap herself out of the gentle intimacy of the moment. "St. Francis of Assisi."

"What?" Judah stood back. "What in the world are you talking about?"

"I'm talking about you. You are too nice, too good. You're a perfect saint."

Judah shook his head and leaned against the stall.

"I'm not perfect, Jamie," he said seriously. "I've made my share of mistakes.

"You mean you have sinned?" Jamie questioned in mock horror. "What did you do? Sing the wrong note at choir rehearsal? Set the table wrong at the church pot luck dinner?"

"No, Jamie. It doesn't matter. What matters is I'm forgiven."

Jamie smirked, glad to get back to reality with Judah. "Spare me," she responded.

"Anyway," smiled Judah, "see, Shadow isn't wild. You can probably feed him sugar by yourself the next time. Once he gets to know you, he's a friend for life."

Jamie looked admiringly at the horse. "He is beautiful," she said.

"Yeah," Judah said, looking at Jamie. "Beautiful."

The young woman blushed. "I've got to go," she said. She grabbed the emptied bowl from Merlin and turned to leave. "See you later."

"Bye, Princess."

Jamie hurried out of the barn. It was a relief to feel the cold wind against her face. *I have got to snap out of this,* she thought. *Seems like every time I'm with Judah I get confused. This is ridiculous. You'd think I had a crush on him or something.*

At such a thought Jamie stopped short and dropped Merlin's bowl.

"No way, heart of mine," she commanded aloud. "Remember the dream I had, chains and all. No way!"

Judah stood in the barn, with the feel of Jamie's hand still burning on his own.

twelve

The air was clear and sweet with the aroma of spring. Jamie breathed in slowly and savored her favorite herald of the new season. The smell of mud and rain and new grass invigorated Jamie's senses. Winter was over!

It was visiting day. Grandmother and granddaughter were on their way to Sadie Atkins's house. Jamie always enjoyed these times with her grandmother. Whoever they visited always had stories to tell, stories that gave Jamie a glimpse into the past.

"I'll drive," Jamie volunteered. "I bet that road up to Sadie's is a mess with mud."

"I will gladly yield the wheel to you, my dear. If we end up in a ditch, it will be your fault."

"Never fear, Richard Petty is here!" Jamie announced.

"Richard who?" Kate asked.

"Never mind," Jamie groaned. "Let's go."

Sadie lived up on Jasmine Hill Road, five miles out of town. The road was paved only part way, and Sadie's was the last house on the route. Jamie carefully maneuvered the car over muddy bumps and ridges. At last they reached the top of the hill. Sadie's house perched on the hill like a lone bird. Despite its peeling paint, the old house had a sturdy look that declared it would be there another hundred years. The windows of the Atkins home were framed precariously by dark green shutters which had obviously seen better days. A couple of vagrant shutters were leaned up against the foot of the house.

Stretched lazily across the front of the building was a long inviting porch.

Katherine and Jamie climbed the porch steps. A pleasant-faced, middle-aged woman greeted the two visitors at the door.

"So glad you could come," the woman said warmly. She smiled at Jamie. "You must be Katherine's granddaughter. How are you feeling? We heard about your fall."

"I'm just fine," replied Jamie. *Good grief,* she thought. *Branded for life. They'll probably put it on my tombstone: Jamie Carrigan: The Girl Who Fell through the Ice.*

"My name's Margret. I'm Sadie's granddaughter."

"How are you holding up, Margret?" Kate gave her a kiss. "Is Sadie behaving herself?"

"Oh, you know Grandma Sadie. She's got a mind of her own!"

"And a clear mind it is, too!" Sadie said indignantly. She stepped out from behind Margret. "Thank your stars I'm not a brainless wonder like old Ed Calhoun. Sits around his house all day, doin' nothin' but watch game shows and talk to his dog. Why, at his age, you'd think he'd be up and about doin' somethin'!"

"Grandma," Margret said gently. "The man is eighty-five years old. He's not a spring chicken! And what are you doing out of your chair? You're supposed to call me when you want to get up!"

Sadie ignored her granddaughter and hit the floor with her cane. "At eighty-five I was helpin' out at the library every Tuesday. Why, I bet Ed Calhoun hasn't cracked open a book in twenty years." Sadie pursed her lips and shook her head. "He came here the other day, looking for all the world like a string of suckers."

"A string of suckers!" Jamie blurted out. All she could picture in her mind was a row of lollipops.

Margret guided Sadie back into the parlor. Kate and Jamie followed them.

"A string of suckers, young lady, refers to a line of fish." Sadie sat down slowly into her rocking chair. "Suckers," she explained, "are good-for-nothing fish with thick lips that stick out like a princess looking for a frog. You can eat 'em, but they're so darned bony it takes about ten to make a mouthful. People used to fish 'em out of the river here and hang a bunch all in a row on a fishing string. Pitiful lookin' thing, a string of suckers, their fleshy lips and skinny bodies just a hangin' there, eyes all staring at nothing. Anyway, I asked old Calhoun what was the matter, did his dog die, or what. Well, he set his mournful eyes on me and said his TV was broken. Said it would be days before it would be fixed." She snorted in disgust. "I guess Vanna White keeps his heart beatin'."

Jamie tried very hard not to laugh out loud, but she couldn't help it. Sadie smiled and peered through her glasses at Jamie, looking her up and down.

"Why don't you do something with your hair?" she asked abruptly. "Hangs there like a mane. You're not a horse, are you? Anyhow, you don't look like a horse."

The surprised young woman gulped and shot a questioning look at Kate. Grandma Kate winked at Jamie in an effort to put her at ease.

"Sadie! You certainly do have a way of speaking whatever's on your mind, don't you?"

"Rude, that's what Margret calls it. She says I'm as

rude as a blue jay in winter when the feeder's full." The old woman pulled her soft blue sweater close and folded her arms across her chest. "And at my age, I don't care. I'll say what I think if I feel like it. Otherwise I'll keep quiet." She smiled at Jamie. "Never mean any harm, though."

The young woman smiled back. She was getting used to Sadie. She hoped Mrs. Atkins would tell some of her stories about Caderville at the turn of the century. Jamie was beginning to realize she had a deepening interest in history and storytelling. Perhaps her time with Grandma Kate was bearing fruit after all. At least if she went back to college in the fall, she knew what her major would be.

Margret walked into the parlor with her coat in hand. "I hope you don't mind, but I'm going to run to the store while you all are here. We need a few things, and I can't leave Grandma alone. Do you mind?"

"Of course not," Kate responded. "You take your time." She got up and walked Margret to the door. "Why don't you stop somewhere and have yourself a nice sandwich, or something?" Kate whispered. "I know you must need a little break from being cooped up here all week."

Margret sighed wearily and nodded. "I sure could use a little pampering myself! Between tending to Grandma during the day and the kids at night, I'm beat!"

"Run along, then," Kate gave her a friendly push toward the door. "We'll be here when you get back."

Kate returned to the parlor to find Sadie and Jamie poring over an old photo album.

"Now what family secrets are you going to tell us today, Sadie?" she asked.

"Pshaw!" Sadie chuckled. "We don't really have too

many skeletons in our closets." She paused and then pointed to a faded picture of a young man leaning against a tree. "Unless you count Jackson Atkins. He was my husband's uncle. He was a gambler. They used to say he'd gamble away his own mother if he was desperate enough. And he usually was. Desperate, I mean.

"Why, my husband used to tell how Uncle Jackson bet their father's chicken coop in a game of twenty-one. And he lost. The next morning, two strangers came and started dismantlin' the coop. Right in front of Jackson's father. He didn't take too kindly to that and run 'em off with a loaded shotgun. He told 'em they had a choice: either all bets were off or their heads were! Well, they high-tailed it out of there and never came back." Sadie sighed. "Not long after, Jackson left the farm and headed for Nevada."

Jamie pointed to an oval photograph mounted on faded brown cardboard. "Who's that?"

A warm smile brightened Sadie Atkins's face.

"That's my Charlie."

"Charles T. Atkins," Kate chimed in. "He was a fine man, Sadie."

Sadie nodded and lay a gnarled finger gently on the picture. "Charlie was a good man, Kate, one of the best. Like your John was." The elderly woman reached over and patted Kate on the hand.

"We met at the county fair in 1910. I was fifteen years old." Sadie looked up and her blue eyes seemed to gaze right back into the past.

"He was showin' a calf at the fair, and my daddy was in the market for a calf. That's where I first saw him. He was brushin' his calf and looked right over at me. The bluest eyes I'd ever seen. He had the Atkins nose, though. You could hang your hat on it. But anyhow, it was love at first sight. We got married two years later."

Kate reached for an old tintype tucked in the back of the album and placed it in Sadie's hand. "Tell Jamie about her."

Sadie fingered the tintype carefully. Jamie leaned forward to get a better look. Despite the deterioration, it was clear that the young woman in the picture had been beautiful. Her hair was swept up in a bun, and her features were delicate.

"Emily Reed," said Sadie.

Emily. That name rang a bell.

"The young pastor and the logger's Emily!" Jamie exclaimed.

Sadie eyes twinkled with amusement at the sight of Jamie's enthusiasm.

"I see you've told her the story," she said to Kate.

"Oh, yes," replied her friend. "Many times. I guess she finds it hard to believe anything exciting or romantic could happen in Caderville."

Sadie shook her head. "There's lots of love stories to be told about Caderville, young lady," she said. "Loves found, loves lost, loves that just plain dwindled away. Like any other town, I suppose."

"What about Emily?" Jamie asked expectantly. "Did your family know her? And did your grandmother really get a letter from the pastor and her? Or is that just a rumor?"

"Whoa, slow down. Give me a chance, and I'll tell you what I know."

Jamie was all ears.

"My family has a long tradition of handing down

stories, stories about the family and the country they live in. My mother and her mother before her could describe the lives and happenings of our people down to the smallest detail. Of course, I never knew Emily. I wasn't even born then! But I know what she was like and what happened to her. I never saw that young pastor, but in my mind's eyes I can see his flaming eyes and curly hair. They said he had a voice like an angel when he preached, and he'd get so fired up with the Word of God that he'd pace around the pulpit, his black curls falling over his forehead, his eyes flashin'.

"Anyway, you know the story. He fell in love with Emily and she with him, and they left Caderville."

"But what about the fire and the letter—"

"Emily's fiancé, Tom Sanders, was a cruel man. Emily knew Tom would try to stop the reverend and her, so they made plans to leave. On the night the pastor usually had his prayer time, he left a lamp on in the church to make it look like he was there. Now, Tom Sanders could burn down a barn in twenty minutes. He knew just what to do. They say he must have sneaked into the church and locked the study door from the outside, thinking the reverend was there. Then he set the church afire. It was burnt almost to the ground by the time anyone even knew it was on fire."

Katherine had disappeared and returned with a cup of tea for Sadie. The old woman accepted it gratefully. The room was quiet for a few minutes as the old woman warmed herself with the tea. Jamie looked around at the antique furnishings. There was a large china closet filled with all kinds of plates, cups, saucers, and pitchers. Some were blue willow, others were creamy white with pink roses painted in garlands along the rims.

Sadie continued her story: "Of course, everyone was mortified. They began planning a funeral until it was discovered that Emily and her few belongings were gone too. Well, they ran Tom Sanders out of town. Mr. Cader rebuilt the church. And that was that."

"What about the letter? Was there really a letter sent to someone from India?"

Sadie adjusted the glasses on her nose and continued. "My grandmother and Emily were—"

"Just let us know when you get tired, Sadie," Kate interjected. "We don't want to wear you out."

Sadie frowned at Kate. "I'd rather be tired from doing somethin' than tired from doin' nothin'.

"Anyway," she began again, "my grandmother and Emily were best friends. One day, several months after the fire, my grandmother received a letter from Emily and the reverend."

Jamie almost fell off her chair with excitement.

"Really?" Jamie exclaimed. "Your grandmother?"

The old woman scowled. "You think I'm making this up?" She sniffed and went on with the story.

"The return address was labeled Serampore, India. They asked that only their close friends be told what they were doing. Well, Grandma made the mistake of telling Luella Haverstraw. Luella was a talker. She could talk and talk. It didn't matter if she was a talkin' to an adult or a child. As long as it was breathin', she was talkin'. When Mama was a child, she used to hide under the kitchen table whenever Luella came to call on Grandma. Once she had your ear, she wouldn't let go!"

Sadie let go a laugh that crackled in the air. "Pretty

soon it was all over town about the reverend and his new bride." Jamie smiled and soaked in the history. Her mind wandered to the young couple who had escaped to fulfill their love for each other. And for God, Jamie guessed. She tried to imagine the trip across the ocean to India. It must have been frightening, but they had had each other.

Sadie saw the look in Jamie's eyes and got up slowly from her rocking chair. She walked over to the china closet that stood in the corner of the room. She opened the glass door and carefully pulled a long manila envelope from beneath a rose-covered gravy boat.

"I haven't shown this letter to anyone in thirty-five years," said Sadie abruptly, "and now I'm ashowin' it to you." Jamie's eyes grew wide with the realization that she was about to see *the* letter. Sadie sat down and painstakingly pulled some papers from the envelope. She handed Jamie a carefully preserved envelope dated 1852.

The young woman fingered the envelope and stared at the words, "Serampore, India." *I'm touching history,* she thought. Then Sadie gave her the letter. The handwriting was graceful but faded. It was hard to make out the words. She squinted, trying to make out the name signed at the bottom.

"That's his name," Sadie explained. "He wrote the letter. Here." She handed another paper to Jamie. "This is a copy of the letter one of my daughters typed out for me years ago."

Jamie eagerly read the letter. She felt a little guilty, as if she were intruding on someone's privacy. The letter briefly described their hurried wedding, presided over by a pastor friend in New York City, and then recounted the tumultuous passage to India.

But one paragraph in particular leapt out at Jamie: "I cannot say what we did was right. I am ashamed and worried that perhaps you will think less of me. Yet I would cross the ocean again for her. Indeed it was out of fear for her life, not mine, that I took her away. As dear as our love is, however, we have both discovered how precious is another treasure we brought with us to this land—the Gospel of our Lord Jesus Christ. The people here flock pitifully around us to see His light, and I am put to tears at the sight of their earnest desire. O that I would handle His Gospel with the care and love that it demands, whether I be in the valleys of the Delaware or the darkened byways of Serampore."

Jamie finished the letter and glanced at the name of its writer. Isaac Weston.

"Weston?" Jamie questioned. "You mean like in—"

"Judah Weston. No, not necessarily any relation to the Westons of Hillside," Kate could read her granddaughter's mind.

"You never know," Sadie piped up. "No one ever asked those Westons about where they came from."

The young woman examined the original letter again. She lightly traced the flowing letters that formed the young man's name.

"Okay, Juliet, I think we've had enough romance for today," Kate said, getting up from her chair. "I think I hear Margret's car. We'd better get going so Sadie can take a nap."

Sadie restored the letters to the safety of the breakfront. A car horn honked in the front yard. Almost simultaneously, a loud crash ripped through the air with a bang.

"Good glory!" Sadie yelled.

Kate ran out to the front of the house. "The roof?" she cried over her shoulder.

Jamie quickly followed her grandmother. She stopped at the sound of Sadie laughing, laughing so hard she was doubled over in her rocking chair.

"It's not the roof!" she cackled. "It's one of those blamed shutters." The ninety-three-year-old woman wiped tears of laughter from her eyes. Kate returned. "It's a shutter," she started to explain, "one of 'em must've fallen off and hit the roof of the porch—" She stopped and looked at Sadie. "What are you laughing at?"

"You!" she crowed. "You ran out of here like Chicken Little on Judgment Day! I haven't seen you move so fast since that time old Bob Henderson tried to ask you out on a date at the church bazaar."

Sadie started laughing again, and this time Jamie joined her. "You should have seen your face, Grandma."

Margret entered with an armful of groceries.

"What's so funny?" she asked.

"You don't want to know," replied Kate. She smiled and gave Sadie a hug. "We've got to go now. You'd better lie down." She turned to Margret. "I think we've worn her out. She's been telling Jamie all about Emily and Isaac."

Margret smiled at Jamie. "Romantic story, isn't it?" she asked. "I used to make her tell me that story over and over."

After thanking their hostess for a lovely time and promising to come again, grandmother and granddaughter drove back down the hill and headed toward home.

"Bob Henderson?" Jamie inquired sweetly.

"Never mind," Kate muttered.

"Is he cute?"

"Jamie!"

thirteen

The canary yellow rent-a-car drove determinedly through Caderville without stopping. A mile from town, it turned left onto a dirt road and soon approached the red mailbox. It hesitated at the mouth of the driveway. The occupants of the car were engaged in a heated discussion, words and emotions flying.

In an effort to buy time, the car passed the mailbox and continued for another mile. The couple reached a temporary truce and bottled up their feelings for the time being. The car turned around and reapproached the red mailbox. It turned up the driveway and came to a stop. Silent and reluctant, the man and woman sat for a moment, enclosed by the brightly colored automobile.

The front door of the house flew open. Jamie ran down the walk with a yell.

"Mom! Dad!"

Ellen took a deep breath and pushed open her door. She threw her arms around her only child and held her tight. Dan Carrigan waited his turn and kissed his daughter on the cheek.

"Jamie girl, you look great!" he said with genuine affection. "I guess all this fresh air is doing you some good after all!"

"Oh, Dad," said Jamie. She studied her parents' faces to see if there was anything different. Since their last conversation, Jamie had never been able to shake the feeling that something was wrong. Right now they just looked tired. Probably tired from the trip.

"Come on inside," Jamie directed. "Grandma's got a big dinner ready for you city slickers."

They laughed and followed Jamie into the farmhouse. Kate gave them a warm welcome, and they sat down to a delicious meal. On the surface, everything appeared to be normal. The family caught up on each other's lives, but in the most general terms. Jamie could sense an undercurrent of tension between her parents; so could Katherine.

In an effort to break the tension, Jamie talked about college. "I think I know what I want to major in," she said excitedly.

Dan and Ellen perked up. "You mean you actually have some direction to go in?" Jamie's father teased.

"Dad!" Jamie exclaimed in exasperation. "I'm serious. I want to study history and literature."

"That sounds wonderful," said Ellen warmly.

"What are you going to do with it?" Dan asked, ever the practical voice of reason.

"I want to write," his daughter replied.

"Write what?"

"Dan!" Ellen scolded. "Write stories, of course, maybe a novel or two, right, Jamie?"

"That's it," Jamie nodded enthusiastically. "Maybe I'll try some journalism too. At any rate, that is the direction I'm shooting for. I want to be a writer."

"Not much money in writing, is there? Unless you write macabre stuff or that lusty love junk that sells today," mused Dan.

"How about macabre lusty junk?" Jamie laughed.

"Very funny," Kate chimed in. "There's enough trash out there today as it is!"

"Actually, Jamie, you were always making up stories when you were little," Ellen reminded her.

"Yeah, like the time you said it was your Raggedy Ann who wet the bed," Dan grinned.

"Dad!"

"No, I don't mean like that! I mean you used to make up stories about princes and princesses and your dog Buffy, things like that."

Jamie sat back in her chair. "I'd forgotten all about that!" she exclaimed. "Maybe it's in my blood to tell stories, like Sadie Atkins and her family."

"Sadie who?" Dan asked.

"Never mind," said Jamie. "Enough about me. What have you two been up to besides work and church?"

Dan and Ellen fell over each other in an effort to sound normal.

"Oh, nothing much," Dan replied. "just the usual. Golfing with the guys. Keeping up with the yard. Dodging earthquakes. I just love California!" he smirked.

"What about you, Mom?"

"Well, Jamie, your dad's been working a lot of overtime lately. So if I'm not working at the church, I'm just sitting at home," her voice cracked. "Excuse me," she said, getting up from the table. "I'm not feeling well. I've got to lie down."

"You go right ahead, dear. It's a long trip from California. You must be exhausted."

Ellen fairly ran up the stairs. Jamie could hear the door close with a bang. She looked over at her father.

"What's going on, Dad?" Jamie demanded. "Something is wrong, and I want to know what it is. Is Mom sick or something?"

Dan Carrigan put his elbows on the table and covered his face with his hands. "No, she's not sick," he said with resignation. He rubbed his eyes and yawned. "I don't want to talk about it right now, okay, Jamie? Besides," he reached across the table and patted Jamie's hand. "It's nothing for you to worry about. She'll be just fine."

Kate didn't say a word but began to clear the table. Jamie sat staring at her father. "I want to know what's going on," she insisted.

"And I said I don't want to talk about it!" Dan snapped. He got up abruptly and stomped through the kitchen and out the back door.

Kate's troubled look only succeeded in fomenting Jamie's anxiety. "Oh Grandma," she whispered. "You don't think it's serious, do you?"

Kate stopped clearing and sat down next to Jamie. "It's obvious they're having problems, but how serious it is I don't know. Only they know, and only they can work it out." She took Jamie by the hand. "You've got to try and stay out of it."

Jamie felt like she was going to throw up. "But Mom looks so upset, and Dad seems like he's going to explode. What if—"

"No 'what ifs' allowed, young lady. Jesus said not to worry about tomorrow, but to let tomorrow worry about itself."

Jamie sighed. "I'll try, Grandma. But it's not going to be easy."

Out in the yard, Dan Carrigan stopped midstride at the sight of Judah leading Shadow out of the barn. "He's a beautiful horse," Dan commented. He took a deep breath of the early evening air. He was glad to be out of the house, away from everybody.

"Thanks," said Judah. He turned the stallion loose in the corral behind the barn. "Judah Weston," he said, offering Dan a handshake.

"Dan Carrigan. So you're Judah. Kate's often spoken of you. Says you're a big help to her."

"I try to help out as much as I can." Judah disappeared into the barn and returned with a saddle. He whistled for Shadow who immediately obeyed, submitting to blanket and saddle.

"So you're Jamie's father," Judah said as he tightened the saddle.

"Yes, Jamie's my little girl." He laughed. "She'd have a fit if she knew I said that."

"You're not kidding," Judah said, half to himself. "Your wife must be beautiful."

"What?"

"Jamie is a beautiful girl. I figure her mom is probably pretty too."

"Uh, yeah, Ellen is—" he spoke haltingly, as if he hadn't thought about it in a long time. "Yes, she is pretty. Like mother, like daughter."

Judah mounted his horse with ease and looked down at Jamie's father. "Nice meeting you, Mr. Carrigan."

"It's Dan. And by the way, how's Jamie doing, anyway? Do you spend much time with her?"

Judah shook his head. "She and I don't see eye to eye on too many things. I try to steer clear of her. Besides, I've been told more than once to mind my own business."

"Sounds like Jamie," sighed Dan. "I don't want to sound like a detective, but what about a guy named Chad Braxton? Kate's mentioned him and—"

"That's another whole subject," Judah replied. Dan noticed a hint of fire in the young man's eyes.

"I've got to go." Judah nudged Shadow and steered him toward the road. "Have a nice evening, sir."

"Thanks." He watched Judah disappear down the road in the muted light of dusk. Shoving his hands into his pockets, Dan turned reluctantly toward the house.

fourteen

Jamie awoke the next morning and for a moment forgot why she felt so down. Then yesterday's scenario replayed itself in her mind and she remembered.

"Mom and Dad," she whispered.

During the night, Jamie thought she had heard the muffled sounds of her mother weeping.

"I'm so glad they came to visit," she said wryly.

At the breakfast table, Dan was missing.

"He went out for the paper," Ellen answered the question in Jamie's eyes.

"Want some pancakes?" Kate asked her granddaughter.

"No thanks," Jamie answered. "I'm not hungry."

"Even if I make it into the shape of a kangaroo? Remember how I used to do that when you were little?"

"No thanks, Grandma." Jamie retreated to the living room.

Ellen followed her daughter and signalled Kate to join them.

"I have something I want to say to you," Ellen said quietly.

Kate sat down. Jamie stayed in front of the fireplace, staring intently into the flames.

"Jamie, I know you realize there is something wrong between me and your Dad. I'm not going to get into the details with you, but I will say this much. Every marriage has its rough spots. We're not immune, and right now we happen to be having a difficult time." Ellen walked over to Jamie and put an arm around her. "I don't want you to worry. Everything will be all right."

Jamie looked at her mother with tears in her eyes. "You don't sound so convincing, Mom. How do you know it's going to be okay? How do you know?"

Ellen turned away, unable to speak. Kate hurried over to her daughter and drew her into her arms. Jamie looked at the two standing there, mother and daughter crying together. She couldn't take it. She bolted from the room.

Jamie ran out of the house and into the field. Her tears blurred her vision. She couldn't see the trees dressed in April buds of promise. Jamie felt as though the foundations of her life were crumbling beneath her feet. Nothing made sense. One minute she was in a ship heading somewhere, then suddenly she was lost on a storm-tossed dingy. There had to be more to life than this. This was crazy.

Just then a horn honked and a car pulled into the driveway. Chad! Jamie quickly wiped her tears and ran to his car.

"Hey baby, how about going for a ride?" proposed the young man.

"I'd love to!" Jamie pulled open the passenger door. "Get me out of here!"

Chad looked quizzically at Jamie, shrugged, and threw the car into gear.

"Your wish is my command!"

The BMW flew out the driveway, barely missing the yellow car that was just pulling in.

By the time they reached town, Jamie had pulled herself together.

"You're out and about early this morning," she said to

Chad.

"Yeah, well, it's Easter break and there's nothing going on. Thought I'd see if you and I could stir up some action in good old Caderville." He glanced at his passenger. "Are you okay?"

"I'm fine," Jamie replied. "Family problems. That's all."

"Don't say another word about it," said Chad. "I make it a policy never to get involved in family problems."

His words seemed a little cold to Jamie, but she didn't really want to talk about it anyway. She opened her window and let the morning air bathe her face with coolness. *Maybe I'm overreacting,* she thought. *Maybe it is just a rough time and they'll work it out. Don't worry, Grandma Kate always said. "The only thing worrying changes is the look on your face. It gives you wrinkles."* Jamie had to agree. Her anxiety over her parents was draining her energy. She decided to put the problem out of her mind. At least she'd try.

Chad stopped at one of the two traffic lights in Caderville. A black Mustang pulled up beside the blue BMW.

"Who's the babe?" asked the driver of the Mustang.

"This is Jamie," Chad replied. "Say hello, Jamie."

"Hello Jamie," Jamie said.

"Hey, a real comedienne!"

"That's kind of a long word for you, Luger."

"Very funny, Braxton. How about a little race?"

Chad's eyes gleamed at the prospect. "And the stakes?" he asked.

"Case of beer?"

"You're on!"

They revved their engines. Jamie grabbed Chad's arm.

"Are you crazy?" she asked incredulously. "We're in the middle of town!"

"Who cares?" Chad laughed. "By the time the local yokel sheriff wakes up and gets his shoes on, we'll be halfway to Lamberton!"

"Oh, great, just great," Jamie said sarcastically. "Drag racing at 8 A.M. in the middle of town. Brilliant. Do you suppose your father will spring for bail?"

"Lighten up! I told you we'd stir up some excitement. And I'm a man of my word!"

"Hey, let's cut the conference," demanded Luger. "Are we on or what?"

"We're on."

They gunned their engines. The light turned green. They took off, tires squealing.

"Yeehaw!" Chad whooped.

Both cars hit seventy in a matter of seconds. Jamie watched the speedometer tip toward eighty. The Mustang straddled the yellow line while Chad maintained the lane. Jamie's heart was pounding. Caderville passed by in a blur. Luckily the road was clear, and in two minutes they were out of town. They raced up the ramp to route 17. The Mustang pulled ahead. Chad chased him for several miles, then gave up with a laugh.

"That Luger! He's got quite an engine under that hood!" Chad slowed the car down to sixty-five. He looked over at Jamie. Her hands were covering her face.

"Are we dead yet?" she asked, her voice muffled by her hands.

"Jamie, lighten up! Wasn't that fun? Didn't your heart beat faster and your palms sweat and your mind swim with that fabulous dizziness that comes from flirting with the edge?"

"The edge of what? A cliff? Chad, you scared me half to death. And besides, I'm not into life-threatening sports."

Chad reached over and put his hand on Jamie's leg.

"I'm sorry, fair maiden," he apologized warmly. "I thought you could use a little excitement, that's all."

"Next time just take me to another horror movie."

Chad took the next exit and turned back toward Caderville. To his surprise and Jamie's mortification, there was a road block on the outskirts of town. The sheriff stood next to his car, arms folded, waiting patiently.

Chad cursed under his breath.

"Great. Just great," Jamie groaned. "I guess the local yokel sheriff got his shoes on after all," she jabbed at Chad.

"Don't rub it in," he muttered.

He pulled over, and the sheriff approached the car.

"Nice little show you put on," he said to Chad.

"Got any proof?" Chad growled.

The sheriff laughed. "Proof! Just about every store owner in Caderville saw you, that's all." He adjusted his glasses and leaned back on his heels, as if he had all the time in the world. "I was at Joe's getting my haircut, when lo and behold, I see a blue BMW and a black Mustang go flying through town. I'd know those two cars anywhere. I figured you'd be coming back. You and I aren't strangers, eh Braxton?"

The sheriff removed his glasses and started cleaning them with painstaking accuracy. "I'm extremely angry with you," he said evenly. "You could have killed someone, including yourself and your buddy there." He peered into the car to see who was with Braxton. "Hey, aren't you the girl who fell through the ice this winter over at Blueberry Lake? Katherine King's granddaughter?"

Jamie nodded. "Jamie Carrigan," she said weakly. *I can't believe this is happening,* she thought. *I'm in trouble with the police. It's California all over again. Grandma's going to kill me. Grandma, nothing!* She sat bolt upright. *Mom and Dad! They're going to throw a fit!*

"Well, I'll tell you what I'm going to do," drawled the lawman. "I won't put any heat on you, young lady. I'm sure you're feeling enough heat as it is." He smiled at Jamie. "You're looking a little green. I know it's none of my business, but if I were you, I'd steer clear of this guy. You're liable to get into trouble."

Jamie sunk into her seat, hoping to disappear.

"As for you, Braxton, here's the deal: I'm slapping you with a hundred dollar fine. Here's your ticket." He handed Chad a slip of paper. "And if I so much as see you spit in the street, I'll land you in jail so fast you won't know what hit you."

Chad took back his license without saying a word. The sheriff tipped his hat to Jamie and returned to his car.

Chad drove slowly through town and back to the King house, cursing all the way. Jamie was shaking her head and staring at Chad as if she had never seen him before.

"You're crazy," she said. "Nuts. Totally gone. The sheriff's right. We could have gotten killed, for Pete's sake. And you know it's going to be all over town, probably before I even get to the front door. I'm doomed. My family's going to kill me."

Chad pulled out a cigarette and lit it. "So you take some

heat from your folks. Big deal! You know something, Jamie. You are always blowing things way out of proportion. So we got caught, big deal! Nobody got hurt."

He pulled the car over to the side of the road, not far from the King property. "I wouldn't do anything to hurt you," he said softly, his gray eyes pleading for mercy. "You are so special."

Jamie looked at Chad and swallowed hard. It was so hard to stay angry at him. He reached over and touched her hair. "Forgive me?" he asked.

"Okay," Jamie whispered.

He leaned over to kiss her.

Blast! A car horn blared through the air with a vengeance. A yellow car pulled up to the BMW.

"I don't believe this," Chad snarled. "Who the—"

"Dad!" Jamie exclaimed.

Jamie's father jumped out of the car. "Jamie, where have you been? I've been looking all over for you! You shouldn't just take off like that. Your mother—"

"My mother is a basket-case, probably because of you!" Jamie fired back at him.

Her words startled him. He stopped and looked at Chad. "Who are you?"

"Chad Braxton," the young man replied. "I'm a friend of Jamie's."

"I bet," Dan Carrigan snorted.

Jamie got out of the car and slammed the door shut. "Thanks for the ride, Chad. I'll walk the rest of the way."

"Whatever you say, Jamie," Chad said. "See you later!" he called out as she walked away.

Dan glared at him. "Jamie!" he bellowed. "I'm talking to you! You get back here!"

Jamie ignored him and kept walking. Dan got back into his rental car and drove slowly back to the house. In the rearview mirror, he could see his daughter's face. His stomach turned as he saw the hurt and anger that was written there.

fifteen

A rousing rendition of "Welcome Happy Morning" filled the sanctuary on Easter Sunday. The people who attended services only on Easter and Christmas helped pack the church. The happy tune and the happy faces of the congregants grated on Jamie's nerves. Her father stood next to her, fidgeting with his tie. Ellen's hands were folded tightly as she quietly sang the hymn. Kate sang with gusto, joy shining on her face.

Jamie looked over at her grandmother. *She must know something I don't know,* Jamie thought. *How can she sing like that when everything is upside down?*

The pastor called the children down to the front of the church. It was time for the children's sermon. The little people walked, skipped, and ran toward the pastor in gleeful anticipation of speaking into the microphone.

"Who knows what today is?" Pastor Jacobsen asked.

Several children raised their hands and answered in unison. "Easter Sunday!"

"Easter Sunday!" Little Tommy Garnett's voice trailed behind the other's, his face beaming.

"That's right," responded the pastor. "Now, who can tell me what Easter is all about?"

"It's about Jesus," five-year-old Clarissa Newcome piped up.

"Jesus," echoed Tommy.

Clarissa gave the little boy a dirty look and continued her exposition. "He got dead because of some bad men

117

and they stuck Him in a hole and on Easter He crawled out of that hole, good as new."

"Good as new," echoed Pastor Jacobsen. "That's right, Clarissa. That's what Easter is all about. We celebrate together because Jesus rose from the dead. Good as new," he said with a smile.

The service continued and Jamie's mind wandered out of the sanctuary and back to the day before. Her parents had tried to reassure her that things were not as bad as they seemed. Jamie had listened politely and decided there was nothing she could do about it anyway. What happens, happens. It's not like they were getting a divorce. At least she hoped not. And at least no one had found out about the drag racing. Not yet, anyway. Jamie looked over at the back of Sheriff James T. Watson's head. Figured he attended First Baptist. He had greeted Jamie that morning with a serious sort of smile. Maybe he was keeping Jamie's involvement to himself. Maybe no one would ever know.

" 'Praise be to the God and Father of our Lord Jesus Christ! In his great mercy he has given us new birth into a living hope through the Resurrection of Jesus Christ from the dead, and into an inheritance that can never perish, spoil, or fade—kept in heaven for you.' " Reverend Jacobsen read the Scripture jubilantly.

"I like those words 'living hope.' In Christ we have a hope that never dies! And what about the word 'new'? He makes all things new! This not only applies to being born anew into the kingdom of God. It applies to our everyday lives as well. He can resurrect our broken dreams, our broken hearts. Why? Because He loves us all dearly. The power of the Resurrection of Christ can affect every area of our lives, if we will let it."

Without her knowing it, the fervent words of the pastor fell like seeds into Jamie's heart and mind.

"What the world gives us can pass away," the pastor continued. "People change, circumstances change. But what God gives us through Christ can never perish, spoil, or fade."

Jamie glanced over at her mother and was in for a surprise. Ellen looked relaxed for the first time since she had arrived from California. There were silent tears running down her face, but Jamie could sense that they were not tears of sorrow. Something the pastor had said was touching Ellen, giving her something to hold on to. On the other hand, Dan Carrigan sat uncomfortably in the pew, acting as if he wasn't listening to what he knew he was hearing.

After the service, Kate King and the Carrigans stopped in the parking lot for a powwow. "I've invited Billy Ritchfield and Judah for Easter dinner today," she announced.

Ellen started to protest but Kate cut her off. "I won't sit around and mope like the rest of you. I love you dearly. I feel your pain. But I trust the Lord. He is faithful. The Lord answers prayer. 'And I'm aprayin' like thunder' as Sadie would say. We could stand for some nice company and light conversation, don't you think?"

Ellen smiled at her indomitable mother. "I'm not going to argue with you, Mom."

Behind Kate's back, Dan mouthed "Oh, great!" and Jamie rolled her eyes. Katherine turned around.

"And you two will have to behave yourselves."

Judah and Billy showed up just as Jamie and Ellen

were putting the finishing touches on the table. The good china and silver candlesticks made a lovely setting for the Sunday dinner. Kate added an arrangement of lilies to the center of the table.

"Aren't they pretty?" She stepped back to admire the flowers.

"That smell reminds me of a funeral home," said Jamie.

"Ditto," agreed Dan.

"Fiddle dee dee," huffed Kate. "I think they smell lovely!"

"I vote for the food smelling lovely," Billy commented from the doorway.

"You would," Jamie laughed. "Mom, Dad, this is my friend Billy Ritchfield. We used to play together whenever I stayed with Grandma."

They shook hands all around. "And this is Judah Weston, my right-hand man," Kate added warmly. "Don't know what I'd do without him."

Judah smiled and joined the group in the dining room. Kate motioned for everyone to take a seat. Jamie ended up between Billy and Judah.

"A rose between two thorns, eh Jamie girl?" Dan teased.

"You can say that again," said Billy admiringly.

"A rose between two thorns, eh Jamie?"

"Cut it out!" Jamie protested.

"So," Dan continued, "what do you two thorns do for a living?"

"I'm a lawyer," Billy replied. "I studied at Harvard and then came back here to open an office."

"Harvard? And you came back to Caderville?" Dan

was incredulous.

"I don't care much for the big city," responded Billy. "Besides, there's a scarcity of good lawyers in this area."

"Here, here," Jamie applauded. "You are a noble and good man!"

Ellen hushed her daughter. "No, Billy, that really is a great thing you've done. I admire a man who thinks of other people besides himself."

Ellen's words made Dan squirm. He turned to Judah. "And you?"

"Mechanic," replied Judah.

"And a good one!" said Kate.

Dan nodded his approval. "There will always be cars to fix, right?"

"He's a cowboy, too, right, Judah?" said Jamie.

Judah's lips curved in a slow, patient smile, and he looked into the young woman's brown eyes. "Yes, I guess you could say that, Jamie."

Jamie looked away. She couldn't look into his blue eyes. Something in them made her feel like a child, like there was something she needed to learn.

"So Jamie," Billy changed the subject, "do you ever have any nightmares about falling through—"

"Billy!" Jamie cried. "If one more person mentions the falling-through-the-ice incident, I think I'll scream!"

Ellen ignored her daughter's aggravation. "That reminds me, Judah," she said. "We wanted to thank you for helping Jamie that day. I'm sure it was terribly frightening. Thank goodness you were nearby to pull her out."

"Let's not forget Billy," said Jamie sweetly. "His tremendously ugly and painfully orange down coat probably saved me from freezing to death, right, Billy?"

Billy straightened up in his seat. "Hey, I never thought of that!" he said brightly. "I'm a hero, and I didn't even know it!"

There was a round of applause for the heroes. The table was cleared away, and the party withdrew to the living room.

"If you'll excuse us, Mom and I are going to do the dishes," Ellen said. "We have some more catching up to do before Dan and I leave tomorrow."

Jamie sat with the men for a while, totally bored with their enthusiastic talk of touchdowns and quarterbacks. Eventually she slipped out of the room and out of the house. She went to the barn and sat down on the top of an old barrel. Through the open doors, Jamie watched the air turn golden as the sun journeyed toward the other side of the western hills. The white farmhouse glowed pale yellow in the retreating rays of light. She could see lights begin to glimmer in the windows of the house.

"Life can be strange," Jamie said to Merlin and Azalia. "You think certain things will stay the same forever, and then wham! Something rocks the boat." She patted Merlin's nose. "I just hope the boat doesn't sink."

In the far corner, Shadow snorted. Jamie approached the black horse slowly and then gingerly reached out her hand to pet him. To her relief, he stood still for her and even nuzzled her hand.

"Judah was right!" Jamie spoke quietly to the horse. "He said once you'd get to know me, we'd be friends for life!" She ventured a hug around the horse's neck. "I wish some of my friendships with people made sense! I'm not so sure about Chad anymore. He's so . . . so careless about things. I can't put my finger on it, but I don't feel right about some of the things he says and does."

"I'll tell you why you don't feel right about Chad," Judah's voice carried from the door of the barn.

"You've got this sneaking business down to a science, don't you," said Jamie.

Judah ignored her comment and pursued the subject of Chad.

"You feel funny because Chad is a self-centered jerk. He doesn't care about you or respect you, Jamie."

"How do you know that?" Jamie asked angrily. She was angry because she knew instantly that he was right.

"The perfect example is the drag race. You could have gotten hurt badly, or even killed. But Chad didn't take that into consideration. He doesn't care about anyone but himself!" It was Judah's turn to be angry.

Jamie walked slowly over to Judah. "How did you know about the race?" she asked weakly.

"Ben told me. And he's fit to be tied. But he doesn't want Katherine to know. It would upset her too much."

"Great. I'm really looking forward to going to work tomorrow." Jamie suddenly felt very weak and very small. It was all too much for her. She hid her face in her hands and began to cry.

Her tears shocked Judah. He hesitated for a moment. Then he awkwardly put his arms around her. "Don't cry," he said. "I didn't mean to upset you."

"It's not you," she said through her tears. "It's everything, it's my parents—"

Judah brushed Jamie's hair out of her eyes and looked at her with concern in his eyes. "I don't know what's going on, but I'm sure your mom and dad can work it out."

Jamie hid her face in Judah's shirt. "I'm not so sure," she said brokenly. "One minute I decide not to worry about it, and the next minute I'm going nuts." She pulled away from him and wiped her face with her sleeve.

"Judah, I'm going to be flat out honest with you. You make me feel like a little kid. You make me feel like there's something I don't know, but that you know. Like you're waiting for me to find out what it is."

Judah looked at her a moment. He ran a hand through his black hair and nodded. "You'll see," he said. "I know you'll find out one day."

An indignant Jamie put her hands on her hips. "And how do you know that, O Great and Mighty Know-It-All?"

"Because I'm praying for you," he replied firmly.

Jamie groaned with exasperation. "Judah," she said matter-of-factly, "thanks for the shoulder to cry on. But let's forget this conversation ever happened, okay?"

Judah bowed to the young woman. "No problem," he said graciously.

"Thank you." Jamie stomped out of the barn.

Judah watched her walk to the house.

Once out of earshot, the tall young man with the cowboy boots had the last word.

"And on top of all that," he said aloud. "Billy's going to be my best man."

sixteen

"Cassie!"

"Jamie, darling!"

The two young women hugged each other. Cassie stepped back to take a look at her friend.

"Well, you don't look like a hillbilly!" she laughed.

"Thanks a lot, Cassie," Jamie said. "Did you think I would turn into a bumpkin or something, living out here in the boonies?"

"Something like that," Cassie sniffed. "But you look great, kind of wholesome-looking, you know?" She ran her fingers through her short, curly black hair. "So who's going to help us with my luggage?"

Jamie looked at the large pile of travel bags and suitcases. "I thought you were staying for three weeks, not three months!"

"Hey, you're lucky! I only brought the essentials," Cassie pouted.

"And it's essential that you have a different outfit for each and every day, right, my friend?"

"Mais oui, darling!"

Jamie picked up two suitcases and started lugging them to the car. Cassie picked up a small satchel. She waited while Jamie put her load into the trunk.

"Don't strain yourself," said Jamie, taking the satchel from her girlfriend.

"I don't want to break a nail!" Cassie cried.

"Oh brother!" muttered Jamie. She grabbed the handle of an extra large piece of luggage and tried dragging it to the car.

"Need some help?" a man's voice inquired.

Jamie turned around. "Hello Chad."

"Hello Chad?" he echoed. "No big hug, no kiss after we faced the threat of death together?"

"What are you talking about?" Cassie asked, dying of curiosity.

"You don't want to know," Jamie muttered.

"She's so reserved, isn't she?" said Chad. "It's what I love about her!"

Cassie started to laugh and Chad joined her.

"Chad, Cassie. Cassie, Chad," Jamie introduced them. "Now if you two are through goofing around, I could use some help."

Chad saluted Jamie and went straight to work. He filled the trunk and most of the back seat with Cassie's things.

"How about we celebrate the arrival of your friend, Jamie?" suggested Chad.

"How sweet!" Cassie purred.

"How about we all take in a movie? My treat!"

Jamie snickered. "His father owns the theater," she informed Cassie.

"I like your style, Chad," Cassie giggled. "We accept."

"Saturday night? Nine o'clock?"

"We'll be there!"

Jamie shrugged. "Why not? We'll see you then, Chad."

Chad reached for Jamie's handed and gently planted a kiss. "Until then, fair maiden."

"You're nuts," Jamie grinned at Chad's handsome face.

"She loves me, can you tell?" Chad sighed dramatically. "See you, Cassie."

Jamie and Cassie slipped into the car, and Jamie drove

to the drugstore.

"Ooh, that Chad is a stunner!" Cassie cooed.

Jamie ignored her.

"I want you to meet Ben, my boss, and see where I'll be working while you sit around and paint your nails."

There was parking right in front of the pharmacy. As they got out of the car, Cassie let out a low whistle. She grabbed Jamie by the arm.

"Be still my heart, I think I'm falling in love! Who is that gorgeous dream walking our way?"

Jamie turned to look down the street. She saw ten-year-old Clarence Sunderman, Jr., sweeping the walk in front of the grocery.

"Cassie, I hardly think CJ is your type," responded Jamie. She kept looking and saw Judah crossing the street. "I don't see anybody. Who are you talking—"

"Him! Him!" Cassie hissed. "He's coming our way! I've just got to meet him!"

With a jolt Jamie realized Cassie was talking about Judah. Judah? A gorgeous dream?

"Hello, Jamie," Judah greeted her as he approached the two women.

"You know him?" Cassie whispered excitedly in Jamie's ear.

"Uh, hi uh, Judah," Jamie stuttered. "This is my friend Cassie Templeton. Cassie, this is Judah Weston. He works for my grandmother."

Judah held out his hand. "Nice to meet you. Welcome to Caderville."

"Why, thank you," Cassie said sweetly.

Jamie stared in amazement at her friend who was drooling over Judah Weston. Then she looked at Judah as if seeing him for the first time. His strong build, his wavy jet-black hair, his pale blue eyes.

Judah began to feel a little uncomfortable, like a bug under a magnifying glass.

"You'll have to excuse me, ladies, I'm on my way to the hardware store. See you later."

"I hope so," Cassie beamed.

Jamie took Cassie by the arm and dragged her into the drugstore. Ben met them in the front of the store.

"Well, well, another beautiful young woman from California." He tilted his head toward the front window. "I see you already met Judah." He extended his hand. "Ben Wheelock, pharmacist."

"Also spy, eavesdropper, and general snoop," Jamie added.

"Jamie!" Ben cried. "How could you say such a thing?" He grinned at Cassie. "Don't believe a word of it!"

"Pleased to meet you," smiled Cassie.

Jamie gave her the grand tour. On their way out, Chad came into the drugstore. Cassie and Jamie acknowledged their date again for Saturday night, waved goodbye, and left for Kate's.

Chad paid for his purchase and was out the door. Ben stood looking after him, twirling his pencil behind his ear. He reached down and fingered the receipt Chad had left behind on the counter. Something wasn't right. The pharmacist had a hunch, a terrible hunch. He hoped he was wrong.

Kate King greeted the girls at the door with a big smile. She showed Cassie to the guest room and served the girls lunch on the side porch. The June air was mild and sweet with the fragrance of the sweet peas thriving nearby.

"Your grandma's a sweetheart," Cassie said. "She really makes me feel at home."

Jamie smiled at her friend. "Yes, she's great. I've really enjoyed my time here."

"So tell me all about these positively beautiful men you've surrounded yourself with! That blond guy is a knock-out. Sounds like he's lots of fun too."

Jamie picked up a cookie and took a bite.

"I'm hardly surrounded," she said dryly. "Chad is sweet, and he is certainly not boring. Now Judah, on the other hand . . ."

"Wait a second," said Cassie, studying Jamie's face. "Chad isn't the guy you wrote me about, is he? In your letter you were so excited about him, he absolutely made you dizzy! What happened? You don't look too excited now." Cassie leaned over with concern on her face. "You know, I hate to sound like your analyst and spoil this nice day, but you look like Courtney Smith looks without her make-up. Kind of sad-looking. What's the matter?"

Jamie smiled. "How is Courtney?"

"Don't change the subject!"

Jamie looked away. "My parents are having problems in their marriage."

"Get outta here, Ms. Carrigan. Your parents? The John and Olivia Walton of Santa Clara? Our very own Cliff and Claire Huxtable?"

"Try Sonny and Cher," Jamie groaned.

"No way," Cassie was vehement. "What makes you think so, anyway?"

"When they were here, Mom looked and sounded awful. Seemed like she was always on the brink of tears. And Dad was real uptight."

"Oh," responded Cassie. "Well, you're probably just making a mountain out of a mole hill. They'll be fine." Cassie reached over and squeezed Jamie's hand. "Don't worry, Jamie. It's going to be all right."

"I hope so."

"Aren't they Christians? I mean like your grandmother is?"

"Yeah," said Jamie. "They go to church and the whole bit."

"Maybe they can work it out then, you know? I thought Christians weren't supposed to have problems like that."

Jamie frowned. "I guess there're just no guarantees."

"Guarantees?" Kate spoke through the screen door. "Guarantees for what?" She opened the door and joined the young women on the porch.

"Marriage guarantees," Cassie said. "We were talking about Christian people and marriage."

"Yeah, Grandma. If Dad and Mom are such great Christians, why are they having problems in their marriage?" Jamie asked accusingly.

Katherine shook her head. "You don't understand, girls. When you become a Christian, Christ doesn't come into your life and make you a sanctified automaton. It's a relationship. We are to walk with Christ, keep in step with Him. If at some point a person gets self-centered and starts focusing on him or herself all the time, you sort of lose your hearing. It's like with each step you're getting farther from the Lord and you can't hear what He's saying. That can turn your life and other relationships into a real mess. No, there are no guarantees for the behavior of the people we live with and love. The only guarantees we have are for God's behavior. He'll always

be faithful, loving, and merciful to His children. I think
those are the only guarantees we'll ever need."

Cassie smiled at Kate. "You sound just like a preacher.
Not a bad one, either!"

"Why thank you, my dear!" Kate replied.

"I just don't get it," said Jamie. "It doesn't make sense
to me." She got up from her white wicker chair and
turned toward Cassie. "I guess we better start hauling
your suitcases in."

"Some of them are really heavy," Cassie said, following Jamie down the steps. "We're going to need a man to
carry them up those stairs. Any suggestions?" she asked
hopefully.

"Judah can do it," Jamie answered without turning
around. She took a smaller case from the car. "He'll be by
to feed the animals later today."

Cassie screamed. "Really?" She grabbed Jamie by the
hand and danced her around the front yard. "This is going
to be a great three weeks!"

True to schedule, Judah arrived to tend the animals.
Kate went out to the barn to invite him in for dessert.

"I better warn you, though," she said in mock serious-
ness. "There may be man-eating sharks in the area!"

Judah blushed and shook his head. "I'm afraid I'm not
much bait, Mrs. K."

Kate smiled and headed out the barn door. "That's what
you think," she said under her breath.

Meanwhile in the kitchen, it was all Jamie could do to
keep Cassie in her seat.

"What has gotten into you?" Jamie asked. "You're
acting like a teenager! You'd think Judah was some
movie star or something! You're acting crazy."

"What do you care how I'm acting? I thought you didn't particularly care for Judah."

"Well, I don't care," Jamie said, beginning to choke on her words. "It doesn't matter to me how you act. I don't care—" As soon as the words were out of her mouth, she realized she did care. A lot.

The kitchen door swung open. "Here we are!" sang Kate. "Judah has agreed to join us for apple pie."

Cassie gave the young man her best smile and motioned for him to sit next to her. He sat down as if he were trying to avoid a porcupine.

"Isn't this cozy!" Cassie exclaimed, pulling her chair closer to Judah.

Judah moved his chair a little to the left, trying to flee Cassie as subtly as he could. Jamie glared at Cassie. Kate turned to the sink, her back to her guests, so they could not see her silently dying from laughter.

It was the longest dessert of Judah's life.

Suddenly, Cassie had a brilliant idea. "Why don't you come with us to the movies Saturday night?"

Jamie tried to kick Cassie under the table but hit Judah by mistake.

"Ouch!" He rubbed his shin.

"What's so painful about the movies?" Cassie asked.

Kate, who by now was seated next to Jamie, nearly choked on her coffee. She finally had to excuse herself from the room.

Cassie looked after her with concern. "Is your grandmother all right?"

Muffled laughter erupted from the direction of the living room.

"She's fine," said Jamie flatly.

"Now, about the movies?" Cassie leaned toward Judah.

"I don't think Judah would want to go," Jamie said, trying to give Cassie a shut-up-already look.

"Why not?"

"Because Chad and he don't exactly get along. To put it mildly."

Cassie laughed. "Why, Judah, you wouldn't be Chad's date! You would be mine!"

Judah pushed his chair away from the table and stood up. "No, I really couldn't," he said apologetically. "I already promised Billy I'd go to Lamberton."

Cassie's eyes narrowed. "Billy? Do we know her?" she turned to Jamie.

The sound of laughter pealed again from the other room. Judah excused himself and hurried out the door.

seventeen

It didn't take long for Cassie Templeton to realize that Judah was not interested; not interested in her, anyway. She gave up the chase and settled down to enjoy her time with her best friend. Jamie introduced her to Billy Ritchfield, and together they formed a threesome. Billy stopped by regularly, games in hand. They played Scrabble, Trivial Pursuit, and Parcheesi for hours into the night. Sometimes Kate joined them, but mostly she sat in her chair and watched. Judah occasionally dropped by, but in the summer he was busy with Shadow, riding him in shows and exhibitions. Jamie missed not seeing him as often, but she figured fair was fair. She hadn't really encouraged him to come around. On the other hand, she could tell he seemed to be avoiding her. Maybe it was just as well. It was hard for Jamie to sort her feelings out.

Chad Braxton was busy working full time at his job in the stock brokers' office in Lamberton. Jamie was relieved. She really didn't want to see him anymore. Ever since the drag race, she had realized what a selfish person he could be. He was hanging out with some new friends in Lamberton. Jamie had met them once at the theater, and they had given her the creeps.

"Want to go for a walk?" Jamie asked Cassie one afternoon. "Sitting on the porch is getting us nowhere."

"A walk? How quaint," said Cassie. She stood up with a stretch. "You know I'm missing three weeks of aerobics for you, darling."

Jamie clutched her heart. "I am truly and deeply touched."

"You're touched all right," said Cassie, thumping Jamie's head.

"Hey, look who's talking," Jamie nudged her. "You're the one seeing a shrink."

"Don't knock Bernie! He's a sweetheart. I get to talk about anything I want. He's a good listener."

The girls headed for the meadow. The summer sun splashed the afternoon with brightness. Blue as a jewel on a king's hand, the sky stretched overhead in a stunning band of color. Dressed for summer, the hills wore variegated greens blending in muted tones. Scattered wild flowers greeted the day with shouts of color, yellows, blues, pinks.

Cassie took a deep breath. "I must admit, the air is definitely cleaner here."

"Does it work?"

"Breathing? Oh, yes, you should try it."

"No, therapy, I mean. Does it help? Do you ever discuss things like, well, the meaning of life?"

"The meaning of life! Jamie Carrigan. I think all this fresh air has gone to your head!" Cassie laughed. "Yeah, I think about life. I think about all the things I want. You know. So many malls, so little time."

"Forget it," said Jamie. "You are in no condition to talk about serious things. You'd better watch your step."

"Jamie, don't you worry about me," retorted Cassie indignantly. "Life and I are doing just fine."

"No, I mean really watch your step—"

Squish. "Too late," Jamie sighed.

"What in the world?" Cassie cried.

"Cow patty. You are now an official member of our family here on the farm. Congratulations!"

Cassie could only shriek in horror. She ran to the house. Jamie ran after her laughing and yelling, "It's not fatal!"

Cassie was sitting on the porch steps, trying to get her shoe off without touching it, when a white car pulled into the driveway. The driver honked at the two young women.

"Hi Billy," they said in unison.

"Want to go over to Sadie's and help Judah and me fix her shutters?"

"Sounds positively exciting," said Cassie limply.

"Yes, we'd love to," responded Jamie. "Just give Cassie time to change her shoes."

"You've got to watch your step around here," said Billy cheerfully, eyeing the offending shoe.

"Thank you, Spock. Your insight and timing are impeccable."

Kate came out the front door with a dish of cookies in her hand. "Did I hear you say you were all going to Sadie's? Can you take these cookies with you? They're her favorite."

"Sure, no problem, Mrs. King."

"I'll carry them, Grandma," said Jamie. "Between Cassie and Billy, those cookies might disappear before we get there."

They piled into Billy's car and drove to Sadie's. When they arrived, Judah was already on the roof pounding nails. He waved with his hammer and then resumed his work.

"Friendly fellow, isn't he?" remarked Cassie.

"When there's a job to be done, he's all business," sighed Billy. "I guess I'd better get up there."

He climbed slowly up the ladder, urging Cassie and Jamie to hold the ladder still. He reached the top and immediately sat down on the roof of the porch.

"What do I do now?" they heard him ask in a shaky voice.

Judah laughed. "Calm down, Ritchfield. You won't fall. Hand me that box of nails and that other shutter."

Sadie came out on to the porch accompanied by Margret. She sat down on the green rocker.

"Hello girls."

"Hi, Mrs. Atkins," said Jamie. "Hi, Margret." Jamie retrieved the cookies from the top of the car and handed them to Sadie.

"Thank you." Sadie's face lit up. "Sugar cookies. My favorite." She looked over at Cassie. "Enjoyin' your stay?"

"Yes," replied Cassie. "I'm really enjoying this country living. Makes for a nice vacation."

"Well, I'm glad. It's a sight better than livin' in the city. Too noisy there. And dangerous, I might add."

"We came to help Judah and Billy with the roof," said Jamie. "I guess we better check and see what they need."

Jamie stepped back and cupped her hands over her eyes.

"What do you want us to do?" she called up to the men.

"Nothing," said Judah. "It will only take two of us. We can handle it."

"William Ritchfield. I thought you said—"

"Oh, never mind," said Billy. "You can help us by just sitting there and looking pretty."

"You're lucky you're out of reach," Jamie retorted.

"I know something you can do," suggested Sadie. "You

can feed Peggy Sue."

"Peggy Sue?" Cassie asked. "Is she a little lamb? A baby calf?"

"A sow," replied Sadie. "A sow as big as a black bear. And twice as mean."

"Sounds like loads of fun," shuddered Cassie. "I think I'll pass."

"We'd love to," said Jamie, pulling Cassie to her feet. "Come on, Cassie. "It's a piece of cake. When you go back to California, you can wow your friends and tell them you actually did some chores on a farm. They'll probably all pass out from shock."

Margret showed them where the feed was and pointed them in the direction of the pig pen. Jamie carried the bucket of food. Cassie reluctantly followed her. When they arrived at the pen, Cassie gasped.

"That thing is huge!" she cried. "I'm not getting anywhere near it!" Peggy Sue snorted up at the girls.

"Come on, it can't get out. Just dump the feed over the side into that trough there," instructed Jamie.

"Why I am listening to you?" complained Cassie. She picked up the bucket and gingerly poured its contents into the trough. Suddenly the sow started squealing and snorting wildly. Cassie dropped the bucket and Jamie screamed. The sow rammed up against the wooden slats of the fence and broke through. Cassie and Jamie took off like lightning, running for the nearest thing they could climb.

Billy was halfway down the ladder when he heard the two women scream. "What in the world?"

"Peggy's loose, I figure," said Sadie calmly. Judah scrambled down after Billy. They rounded the corner of the barn in time to see Cassie and Jamie frantically clambering over the side of Judah's truck. Peggy Sue was desperately trying to reach them, snorting and jerking and jumping as best she could.

"Do something!" Cassie screamed.

Jamie was doubled over, laughing hysterically.

"Go get the hammer and nails," Judah told Billy.

"Gladly," he said, eyeing the sow.

Judah grabbed a stick and a handful of feed and herded the animal back to its pen. Billy brought him the hammer and nails, and Judah quickly repaired the fence.

Billy helped Cassie and Jamie out of the truck.

"Piece of cake. Wow your friends." Cassie seethed. "Jamie Carrigan, I'll never forgive you. We almost got killed."

Jamie was still choking from laughter.

Billy tried to maintain a straight face. "It's not funny, Jamie. Cassie was really frightened." He cleared his throat. "Imagine your epitaph." He recited: "Our friends have departed/ We all know how/ They were hit and run over/ By Peggy Sue Sow."

Jamie fell to the ground, holding her sides. "Stop!" she cried, "It's too much!" Tears of laughter streamed down her cheeks.

"I am not amused," said Cassie, fighting a smile. She climbed up on the porch and sat down.

Judah returned, hammer in hand. "Are you two all right?" he asked.

Jamie nodded, gasping for breath. Cassie rolled her eyes. "I'm fine. Miss Carrigan seems to be having a breakdown."

"Honeysuckle," said Sadie.

"What?" All eyes were on Sadie.

"Someone must be wearing honeysuckle. Drives Peggy Sue wild. She just loves it."

Cassie looked a little pale. "I'm wearing a perfume that is a blend of honeysuckle and musk."

"An expensive perfume, I bet," reported Jamie.

"Very," said Billy. "It almost cost Cassie her life."

At that, Jamie and Billy broke up laughing.

"My father used to have a sow just like Peggy Sue," reminisced Sadie. "Her name was Belinda. One day, my cousin Orville and his wife Kitty came up from the city for a visit. Kitty was real prim and proper and citified. Well, unbeknownst to us, she was wearin' honeysuckle perfume. Belinda got one whiff of that and broke out of her pen. She chased Kitty clear to the other side of the field. Knocked down nearly an acre of corn before we could stop her." Sadie slapped her knee and let out a laugh. "An acre of corn!"

Cassie shot Jamie a dirty look.

"And then there was the time Belinda went after the judge's wife. Marilyn Parker, that was her name. She came one day to bring over some molasses for my mother. Well, sir, Belinda got loose and chased that woman up a tree. Never saw a woman her age climb a tree before, but Marilyn Parker did it. And fast. She would've made a monkey proud."

Sadie stopped for a moment, remembering. "Mother had to call the fire department. Mrs. Parker wouldn't let my father get her down on account she thought he'd drop her. My father never liked the judge. You know, come to think of it, Marilyn wasn't even wearin' perfume. I expect Belinda chased her out of sheer meanness."

"I'm getting a headache," said Cassie.

"I'll drive you girls home," Billy volunteered.

"We're done with the shutters, Mrs. Atkins," said Judah. "They shouldn't be falling down any more."

"Thanks so much, boys," said Sadie. "I don't know how to thank you. My grandsons couldn't hammer a nail straight if their lives depended on it."

Judah smiled and put his tools back in the truck.

"Come again!" Sadie called after the girls. "And thank Kate for the cookies!"

That evening after they ate, Jamie and Cassie settled in the guest room to talk. Jamie hugged a pillow and watched as Cassie carefully painted her nails. Her lips pursed with concentration, Cassie stroked the color on with admirable precision.

"You ought to go into business," said Jamie. "Nails By Cassie."

"Very funny, darling, but don't laugh. There's money to be made in the beauty business."

"What is that awful color, anyway?"

"Sparkling fuchsia."

"Good grief," Jamie responded.

"It happens to be a very hot color right now," retorted Cassie. "You really should try it."

"No thanks," Jamie replied. "You know I hate fussing with my nails."

"Obviously," said Cassie, wrinkling her nose at the sight of Jamie's short nails.

Jamie leaned back and took a deep breath. "Cassie?"

Cassie looked up from her nails and eyed her friend. "Now what? You've got that 'I need to ask you a very important question' look on your face."

Jamie nodded. "What was it like when your parents went through their divorce?"

Cassie's eyebrows shot up and she leaned back on the post of the bed. "Wow! Talk about left field."

"Come on, tell me how it was. How did you feel? What happened?"

Cassie sighed and resumed her painting. "Well, I was twelve at the time. Mom and Dad had been fighting on and off for a long time. Seemed like every fight got worse until one day it stopped."

"It stopped?"

"Yeah, they stopped talking altogether. The silence in the house was unbearable. Shortly after that, Dad left. With his baby-faced secretary on his arm, if you know what I mean." Cassie snickered. "You'd think he'd have had more imagination than that! Seems like it's always the secretary. Not very original."

Jamie felt sick to her stomach. "What about your mom?"

Cassie frowned and replaced the brush in the bottle.

"Mom was devastated. She cried a lot. For a long time." Cassie looked away for a moment. "I think that was the hardest part," she said, her voice trembling. "To see Mom suffer so much. I used to hear her at night in her room, trying to cry in her pillow so we wouldn't hear her. It was awful." Cassie cleared her throat. "But she got over it. She pulled herself together and got on with her life. She's a very together lady. She always looks put together, from her hair to her nails. Very stylish. She's got her friends and her clubs and her boyfriends."

Jamie smiled. "What about you?"

"What about me?"

"Did you get over it?"

"Of course," Cassie said simply. "I made up my mind to hate my father. That helped take away the hurt and betrayal I felt through all that garbage. Bernie says I need to get rid of the hate, but so far it works just fine."

Jamie swallowed hard. "I don't know, Cass. That doesn't sound like the right way to deal with something like that."

"And what do you know about it?" snapped Cassie. "You don't what it's like to wake up in the middle of the night and feel like the whole universe is falling apart. You don't know what it feels like to be so lonely you don't think you can get out of bed in the morning." Tears were streaming down her face. "I used to feel like it was my fault, like if maybe I was a nicer kid or better student, my parents would have stayed together. I felt like the ugliest, dumbest kid in the world. It was awful.

"Oh, now look what you made me do! I've smeared the polish on my thumbnail." Cassie wiped her eyes and grabbed the polish remover. She blinked away her tears and concentrated on her nails.

Jamie reached over and put her arms around her friend. "I'm sorry," Jamie whispered. "It's just that I'm afraid my parents—" She couldn't say another word.

Cassie closed her bottle of color and held Jamie at arm's length. "I told you before, don't worry about it. Besides, you're an adult now. It might not be so hard to deal with when you can understand what's going on." She got up from the bed and blew on her nails. "All this gloomy talk has got me starved. Let's go beg your grandmother for a late night snack."

Jamie followed her friend down the stairs. Kate greeted

the two young women in the kitchen. "What long faces!" she exclaimed. "Who died?"

"True love," said Cassie ruefully. "We were discussing an obsolete concept."

"Oh my!" said Kate, rising to the occasion. "That's simply not true!"

"Oh no," muttered Jamie. "Here she goes."

"True love is God's love. And that never dies. Never! He says in His Word He'll never leave us or forsake us. And it's true."

"Well, Mrs. King, that sounds real nice, but I can't get into that," said Cassie. "I guess I just don't see how that fits into real life."

Kate smiled. "Well, I shall pray you come to see it. He loves you Cassie. Just the way you are."

"Grandma!" Jamie sighed.

"No, Jamie, I like to hear your grandmother talk about her faith. It's nice."

Jamie rolled her eyes. "You shouldn't have said that."

"Let's make some sandwiches, and I'll tell you all about it," said Kate enthusiastically.

"Deal!" said Cassie.

"Oh boy," lamented Jamie.

Kate patted her granddaughter on the cheek. "Get out the mayonnaise, dear. This is going to be fun!"

The faithful clock on the mantel in the darkened living room kept pace with the approach of midnight. Light from the kitchen vainly tried to reach around the corner of the hall to spread its warm glow, its edges swallowed by the shadows of nighttime. In the kitchen, the unseen light of another kind shone brightly around the three women at the table, the air dancing with words of love and hope and promises kept.

All too quickly, Cassie's vacation ended. "I can't believe three weeks is over already," she sighed. She straightened her large sun hat and put on her sunglasses. Her luggage was being loaded on the train.

Jamie gave her a big hug. "I'll miss you, Cass. I'm so glad you came."

"I really enjoyed myself," said Cassie. "This simple country living almost has me hooked!"

"Good!" exclaimed Billy. "Why don't you move here?"

Cassie looked over the top of her sunglasses. "I said almost, Billy dear."

Kate gave Cassie a kiss. "Any time you want to stay with me, you just give me a call."

"You have a safe trip, now Miss Templeton," Judah shook her hand.

Cassie motioned for Judah to come closer. "You keep an eye on that girl," she said quietly, pointing to Jamie. "She is one of a kind."

Judah nodded. "I will," he replied. "That's a promise."

Jamie blushed and gave her friend another hug. "Thanks for the listening ear, Cassie. You are the best."

"I'm only going to California," Cassie protested. "You all make it sound like I'm falling off the edge of the earth!"

"Well," mused Billy, "from what I've heard about those earthquakes, you know, and California . . ." He made a motion with his hand. "Splash! Right in the Pacific Ocean."

Cassie batted him on the head, waved goodbye, and boarded the train.

eighteen

"Hello, Jamie," Chad called to her as she walked down Main Street.

"Hi Chad. What's with the Jeep?" Jamie asked. She stepped over to the Jeep and looked inside. "Looks new. Tired of the BMW?"

Chad patted the steering wheel. "It's my Dad's latest toy. Thought I'd give it a spin. Want to come?"

"Sorry. Can't do it. Ben's going out for the afternoon so I'll be covering the store myself."

"Oh," said Chad thoughtfully. "So you'll be closing up the place?"

"No, my grandmother's going to do it! Of course I'll be closing up the place!" She gave him a quizzical look. "Why do you ask?"

"Uh, well," Chad cleared his throat. "I was wondering if you wanted to have dinner over at the diner. I could pick you up after work."

"I don't know, Chad, I'm kind of tired today, and I know by tonight I'll be bushed. Maybe another time."

"Why Jamie Carrigan! If I didn't know better, I'd say you were trying to avoid me!" He pursed his lips. "I'm hurt."

"Save your puppy dog face for the other girls, Chad. I'm immune," she laughed.

"Please, Jamie, pretty please with a hot-fudge-sundae-I-know-it's-your-favorite on top?" He gazed into her eyes.

There it was again. There was something about Chad's face that was different. She just couldn't put her finger on it. What was it? Maybe his eyes? Did the familiar gray eyes seem a little cloudy or something?

"Come on, Jamie," Chad pleaded. "We'll just go to the diner. No big deal!"

"Okay," Jamie gave in. "I'm through here at five."

"Great!" Chad grinned. "See you then!"

Jamie watched him drive away in the new Jeep. His grin stayed fixed in her mind. It had seemed kind of strange. In fact, it hadn't looked like Chad at all.

I must be tired, she thought.

Jamie returned to the pharmacy. Ben gave her the key and instructions for closing up shop. "Now the meeting I'm going to is in Lamberton. It should be over by four. Here's the phone number in case something comes up. If the meeting ends on time, I'm going fishing. So you won't see me until tomorrow. Any questions?"

Jamie couldn't think of any. "Don't worry about a thing."

"I won't," Ben smiled. "Thanks to you!" He walked toward the door. "Just bring the key with you tomorrow," he said over his shoulder.

"Okay. Hope you catch a big one!" she called after him.

Jamie busied herself around the store, dusting shelves and waiting on customers. No prescriptions could be filled, but there were plenty of other things to do. It seemed like every customer wanted something they couldn't find themselves, and everyone wanted to know where Ben was.

"Yoo hoo," a voice sang across the aisles to Jamie. "Young lady!"

Jamie looked up from the cash register to see a plump woman dressed in purple. She was signalling to Jamie to join her in the second aisle.

"Can I help you?" asked Jamie.

"Shhh!" the woman hushed her. "Not so loud!"

Jamie looked at the woman in surprise. "What seems to be the problem?" she asked quietly.

"Well," spoke the woman in a loud whisper. "I've run out of dye for my hair."

Jamie looked at the woman. Her hair was jet black except for the tell-tale gray roots.

"How can I help you?"

"I can't seem to find the brand I always buy." She looked furtively up and down the aisle. "I'm glad Ben's not here. I never buy it when he's around. He's such a snoop and a talker. No one knows, of course, that I dye my hair. Naturally, my hair is not all that gray. I really just need to touch it up." She primped her hair and handed Jamie an empty box of the dye she used. "Here it is," she whispered. "See if you can find it."

Jamie began her search. *I feel like James Bond,* she thought. *Any minute someone with a briefcase machine gun is going to turn down this aisle and let us have it.*

"Hurry!" hissed the woman. "I can see Alma Stack walking down the street! She's probably coming here!"

Jamie found a box behind a package of blond dye and handed it over to her customer. The woman nodded toward the cash register. "Let's go."

Jamie rang up her purchase and put the secret in a bag. She handed it to the woman, who sighed with relief.

"You must be Kate's granddaughter," the woman smiled.

"That's right. I'm Jamie Carrigan."

"You're the one who fell through the ice this past winter, aren't you?"

"Yes, ma'am, that's me," Jamie sighed.

The woman shook her head. "I used to skate. That is until Benjamin Wheelock nearly killed me."

Jamie coughed, trying not to laugh. "You must be Violet Cranberry."

"Yes, dear, that's me," she smiled and primped her hair again. She leaned close to Jamie and whispered in her ear. "Benjamin had quite a crush on me, don't you know? But of course, after the accident, it was all over between us." Violet turned to leave. "Now don't you tell anyone now, okay dear? I mean about my hair, of course."

Jamie nodded. "Not a word!"

"Bye now!"

She watched the lady in purple walk grandly out the door. "Yoo hoo! Alma!"

Jamie smiled and leaned against the counter. She was really feeling at home in Caderville.

There was no letup in customers for the rest of the afternoon. At five o'clock, it was with great relief Jamie finally put the closed sign in the window. She locked the door so no one could slip in for one last purchase. She was about to lock up the cash register when there was a knock on the window. It was Chad.

Rats! She had forgotten about their dinner date. *What I'd really like to do is go home and soak in a hot tub,* she thought.

She opened the door for Chad and let him in.

"I just have a couple of things to do, and I'll be right with you," she said.

"Take your time," he smiled.

Jamie locked the cash register and then walked to the back of the store. Ben always double-checked the back room where the drugs were kept. A couple of cabinets he kept under lock and key. Jamie quickly scanned the room. Everything looked in order. She turned to leave and nearly bumped into Chad.

"What are you doing, Chad?" she asked. "I didn't even hear you follow me. You scared me half to death!"

"I'm sorry, Jamie," he said. His voice sounded thin. "I didn't mean to frighten you."

She looked at his face. His pupils were dilated and his breathing was loud, almost labored. Jamie felt prickles of fear rise on the back of her neck.

"We can go now, Chad," she said weakly. "I'm finished."

He fervently shook his head. "No, we can't go now. You're not finished. We have to pick up a few things for our journey."

Jamie laughed nervously. "We're just going to the diner, Chad."

"No," he said sharply. Then his voice softened. "We're going to our castle, you and I. And we'll need some very special supplies."

He pushed his way into the back room. "We'll need some footballs and yellow jackets."

"What?" Jamie's voice trembled.

"Uppers and downers, come on, pills. You know where they are. Get them."

"You mean—" Jamie's brain was starting to freeze with fear.

Chad snorted in disgust. "Amphetamines and barbiturates, if you must have the technical terms. Now find them. We're going to need them."

"But I don't have the keys—"

"Hurry up!" the man fairly shrieked.

Suddenly, the sound of footsteps clacked hurriedly down the main aisle of the store.

"What's going on around here?" Ben Wheelock demanded. "What are you doing back here, Braxton?"

"Ben!" Jamie cried.

As Chad turned slowly around, he pulled a small pistol from inside his shirt.

"Calm down, Wheelock. We're merely shopping for supplies."

Ben looked down at the pistol. "Have you gone mad?"

"Shut up!" A smile spread over Chad's face. "How good of you to stop by and lend us a hand." He grabbed Jamie and moved away from Ben. He directed Ben with his pistol. "Give us all the pills you've got. You know what I mean."

"I'll give you whatever you want, just let Jamie go."

"No!" Chad hissed. "She's coming with me."

Ben hesitated. He looked at Jamie. She was shaking with fear. "Let her go!"

"Don't make me angry, Wheelock!"

"Ben, please, just do as he says," whispered Jamie.

The druggist took two keys from his pocket and reluctantly unlocked two of the cabinets. He removed two bottles of pills and handed them over to Chad. Chad grabbed them and in one quick motion hit Ben on the head with the butt of the pistol. Ben fell to the floor. He wasn't moving.

"No!" Jamie screamed.

Chad jerked her back and threatened her with the gun.

"Be quiet, or I'll do something worse." He handed her the jar of yellow pills. "Open it up and take one."

"No way," Jamie shot back. At the sight of Ben lying on the floor, she was beginning to burn with anger.

"Just say no. Pity that's not going to work this time." He pointed the gun toward Ben's head. "If you don't do as I say, I'll just have to kill Mr. Wheelock. Now that would make it your fault, wouldn't it?"

Jamie opened the bottle with shaking hands.

"Now just take two," Chad said softly. His voice was suddenly sweet. "It's just to relax you."

Jamie looked at the pills in her hand.

"Take it," he said sternly.

Jamie swallowed the pills. She looked down at Ben. Tears streamed down her face.

Chad took her by the hand and hid the pistol behind her back. "We're going to leave now. Walk very carefully out of the store. Lock the door. Then we'll get into the Jeep."

Jamie obeyed. There were people in the street, but the cold nozzle of the gun reminded her to act normally. She climbed into the Jeep with Chad close behind.

"Hold your hands out."

Jamie obeyed.

"That's a girl." He quickly tied a rope around her hands.

Chad started up the Jeep. He laughed out loud. "Broad daylight," he chortled. "Everyone sees us and no one knows!" He shivered with excitement. "I love the edge," he whispered gleefully. He threw the Jeep into gear and drove through town, obeying the speed limit.

Jamie tried to see where Chad was taking her. He drove

out the southern end of town and followed River Road for several miles. Jamie was starting to feel drowsy. She felt her head drop to the back of the seat. *No, no, stay awake, awake.* It was too hard to keep her head up.

Chad slowed down and turned onto a dirt road that was obscured by trees and overgrowth. Jamie didn't recognize the road. It was difficult to keep her eyes focused. The road climbed the side of a mountain, turning into a narrow path barely wide enough for a vehicle to drive on. The Jeep jerked along the rough terrain, helping to keep Jamie awake. After what seemed like hours, Chad pulled up to a cabin hidden among a cluster of evergreens. There was a motorcycle parked in front.

"Here we are, fair maiden! Our very own home away from home. Our castle." Chad opened the passenger door and helped Jamie out of the Jeep. Her legs were like rubber, and she fell against him.

"Whoa, darling! Not in public!" He propped her up and led her to the front door of the cabin. After lifting up the large slat that barred the door, Chad whisked Jamie up into his arms, carrying her over the threshold.

"Here we are!" he cried. He put Jamie down. With a dramatic sweep of his arms, Chad showed off the interior of the cabin. "Like it?" he asked anxiously.

Jamie couldn't answer. She struggled with the rope around her wrists.

"Now, now, leave those on, my dear. We wouldn't want any accidents to happen." He ran over to a dilapidated coffee table. "Look!" he said excitedly. "Look what I bought for you!"

He held up a Scrabble game. Jamie shook her head. *This isn't happening,* she thought. *I must have a fever. I'm hallucinating.*

"You look like you need a nap," Chad said matter-of-factly. "I guess you not only can't hold your liquor, you can't hold your barbs. Poor baby."

He led her over to an old cot and ordered her to lay down. As she put up her feet, he pulled out some rope from underneath the cot. "Now be a good girl and let me tie your feet together." He knelt down to secure the rope around her ankles.

Jamie mustered what strength she had and kicked Chad in the face. He flew into a rage.

"Don't do that! You hurt me!" His face turned bright red. The veins on his neck popped out and throbbed. He raised his hand to hit Jamie across the face. She closed her eyes and stiffened in anticipation of his fist.

No fist came. Jamie opened her eyes. Chad was shaking his head, smiling crookedly at her. "No, no, my dear. I mustn't hurt you. You must be in top shape for our journey."

"Chad, what are you talking about?" Jamie's speech was slurred. "You're crazy. You're on something, aren't you?"

Chad laughed and commenced tying Jamie's feet together.

"Yes, my dear, I have found the way to paradise. And I want you to come with me." He finished his job, pulling the roped tightly. "Some people call it Snow," he said. He paused, folding his arms across his chest. "Let's see, now," he searched his memory. "Some call it Lady, the Big C, Flake." He leaned over Jamie. "I prefer to call it the Ultimate Edge."

Jamie was losing the battle to stay awake. Chad covered her with a blanket. "Sweet dreams," he whispered. "While you nap, I'll fix dinner." He stood over the sleeping young woman for a few moments, perched like a vulture. He wiped his running nose with a white hand-kerchief elegantly emblazoned with the letters CB.

nineteen

Ben groaned. He sat up slowly, rubbing his head.

"Jamie," he uttered her name. Looking at his watch, he figured he'd been lying there long enough for Chad to disappear without a trace. Grabbing the back of a chair, Ben pulled himself to his feet. He plucked up the receiver of his phone and dialed the police.

Ben quickly related the incident to Sheriff Watson.

"You'd better go to Kate's and break the news to her," the sheriff said. "I'll send John over to check out your place, Ben. I'm on my way to Braxton's."

"So am I," Ben seethed, banging the receiver down.

When Kate opened the front door, she knew something was terribly wrong. "Ben? Is it Jamie?"

"Come and sit down, Kate."

"Ben? What is it? Just tell me!"

"Kate," Ben began to choke on his words. "Jamie is missing."

"What?" Kate gasped. "What are you talking about? I don't understand!"

"Mrs. K!" Judah's voice sounded from the kitchen. He walked into the living room. "I knocked but you didn't hear me. I was wondering if—oh, hello Ben." Judah looked at Kate. "What's wrong?"

Kate could only respond by breaking down, a torrent of tears covering her face.

Ben stood up. "It's Jamie, Judah. She's missing. Chad Braxton's got her. He came to the store. He knocked me out." Ben rubbed the back of his head. "I couldn't help her. I let him get away," he said angrily.

Judah's face paled for a moment, his mouth formed a grim straight line. "Braxton," Judah spat the name. He headed for the door. Ben followed him. Judah turned and stopped him. "You stay here, Ben. Kate's going to need you. Call Reverend Jacobsen and Billy and anyone else you can think of."

Ben nodded. "Watson's over there now. Have him call me with the plan of attack."

Kate looked up at Ben. "I've never been this frightened, not since the day we took John to the hospital. God gave me peace then. He'll give me peace now. I just wish I could have done something. I tried to tell her, but—" Tears began to flow again.

Ben put his arms around her. "Now, Kate, you've got to be strong. You know your faith has gotten you through a lot of things. You'll get through this."

Jamie's grandmother shook her head. "No, Ben. It's not my faith that sees me through. It's the Lord."

Just saying those words aloud gave Katherine a surge of strength. Her face brightened. "I don't have to rely on my own strength, Ben. I can rely on His!"

Ignoring the confused look on Ben's face, Katherine continued. "I have always told Jamie that God will never leave us or forsake us. And she's heard Reverend Jacobsen's sermons. We'll just pray that Jamie remembers these things. Yes! That is our plan of attack, Mr. Wheelock. Start praying for God's Word to come to Jamie wherever she is. It's what she needs right now. I know God will hear our prayers."

Ben nodded. "Okay Kate. Whatever you say."

Kate took a deep breath and got up from the sofa.

"I've got to call Ellen and Dan first," she said.

She walked into the study and picked up the phone. "Be calm, Kate," she said to herself. She dialed California. "Hello, Dan Carrigan," Jamie's father answered the phone.

"Dan, this is Kate. Where's Ellen? Tell her to get on the other phone."

"What's the matter, Kate?" Dan asked. "You sound upset."

"Get Ellen."

The other line clicked. "Hello, Mom, what's the matter? It's Jamie, isn't it? What happened?"

"She's missing. Chad Braxton has kidnapped her."

The silence at the other end of the line cut Kate's heart.

"The police are looking for her, and we're praying and—"

"We'll catch the next flight out of here," said Dan hoarsely.

Dan hung up the phone and rushed to the room where Ellen stood. She was clinging to the phone, hands shaking, tears streaming down her face. Dan took the phone from her and gathered his wife in his arms.

"It's okay, Ellen. It's going to be okay. You go pack some stuff while I call the airport."

Ellen composed herself and headed for the bedroom.

"If anything happens to her, I'll—" Dan stood alone in the room. Everything seemed to crash in around him. Thoughts of Jamie swarmed his mind. He could see her take her first step. Her first day of school. The look on her face on Christmas morning. Walking down the country road at Grandma's, hurt and angry. "Oh, my God. If anything happens to her . . ." He stopped himself and shoved his thoughts aside. "We're coming, Jamie," he said picking up the phone. "We're coming."

Kate returned to the sofa. Ben began to make the other phone calls. Billy was the first to arrive, followed by Kate's friend, Louise Hanson, and Pastor Jacobsen.

"Everyone in Caderville's praying," spoke the pastor.

"The whole valley," added Billy. "They're going to find her. Don't worry, Mrs. King."

Kate smiled. "How can I worry when the saints are storming the throne?"

"On the way over here, I got to thinking about some verses in Psalm 46," said Louise quietly. "Would it be okay if I read them to you?"

Kate nodded. "Please do."

" 'God is our refuge and strength, an ever present help in trouble. Therefore we will not fear, though the earth give way and the mountains fall into the heart of the sea, though its waters roar and foam and the mountains quake with their surging.' "

Pastor Jacobsen took Kate by the hand.

"He's sending help, Katherine. I just know it."

Judah sped over to the Braxton residence. The sheriff's car was parked in front. Judah burst through the front door. Sheriff Watson stood in the large front hall with a piece of paper in his hand. The Braxtons stood with him, looking terrified.

"What have you got?" Judah demanded. "What's going on?"

"Hold on a minute, Judah. We're handling it."

Joseph Braxton spoke up, perspiration running down his face. "He left me a note," he explained, pointing to the paper in the sheriff's hand. "Said he was borrowing the

Jeep to take Jamie shopping in Lamberton."

"Jeep?" Judah asked.

"Yes," said Joseph. "It's new. It's green with black interior . . ." His voice trailed. "I am so sorry about all this. I should have seen it coming."

"What do you mean?" the sheriff asked sharply.

"Well, my son, Chad," Joseph Braxton's voice broke. "He's been acting strangely the last few days. Kind of spacey, volatile. Even paranoid."

"Drugs?" the sheriff snapped.

"I'm not sure, but yes, I think so."

Judah headed out the door. The sheriff followed him.

"Hold on, Judah. I've called the troopers and the boys in Lamberton already. I've got an APB out on both Chad and Jamie. He's probably hiding out somewhere in Lamberton. There's nothing much we can do but wait."

"Yeah, well you can wait all you want." Judah jumped into his truck. "I'm looking for Jamie."

"Judah, you just hold on a minute. We will handle this. I've got my men out questioning people. We'll see if we can dig anything up. In the meantime, you stay out of this. Go back to Mrs. King's place. I don't want you running around half-cocked. I'll call you as soon as we hear anything."

Judah punched the steering wheel. "I'm warning you, Judah. Stay out of the way. We'll handle it."

Jamie awoke to see Chad sitting at a table with a plate of sandwiches.

"It's about time, Jamie! I want to feed you dinner. I've so many things to do," he chattered. "So much to do, so little time!"

Jamie's head was clear and she struggled to sit up.

"Let me help you," Chad said sweetly.

"Get away from me!" Jamie screamed. She pulled her legs over the side of the cot and sat up herself. "Get away from me!"

"No, no! That will never do!" Chad clucked. He picked up a cloth and gagged the young woman. "I can't think straight when you're screaming!" He shook his head. "Just for that, no lunch for you!" he pouted.

Jamie tried to stand up. She fell to the ground with a thud. Chad grabbed her and dragged her across the room. He propped her up against the wall.

"Stay, Sheba!" He snickered. "Get it? Sit, Sheba, heel."

Chad busied himself on the other side of the room. Jamie felt panic rising within her. This guy was crazy. He was obviously on something. What was he talking about before? A ticket to paradise? What did he call it? Snow? The Big C? She'd heard those words somewhere.

It hit Jamie like a blow to her stomach. Her blood ran cold. Cocaine. The man was hooked, and he was going to take Jamie with him.

Her eyes darted around the room. There were all kinds of supplies, magazines, books, food. Chad had fully stocked the place, as if he were planning on staying for a long time.

Chad walked over to Jamie and knelt down beside her. His hands were shaking.

"A friend of mine is going to drop off our ticket to Paradise, at an undisclosed location, of course. I must go now and pick it up." He rubbed his hands together. "And of course I'll take the motorcycle. The fools in town will be looking for a green Jeep." Chad convulsed with cruel laughter. "Besides, the idiots think we're in Lamberton, shopping at the mall."

Suddenly serious, Chad leaned close to Jamie.

"You know that old question everybody discusses in high school, the one about if a tree falls in the forest, and there's no one to hear it, does it make a sound?"

Jamie looked at him in confusion and fear.

"Well," he continued, "I've been thinking. Let's do a little experiment. You like experiments, don't you?" He removed the gag from around her mouth. "While I'm running my little errand, you can scream all you want. There's no one around here for miles. The question is, will your screams make a sound?" He laughed hysterically and hugged himself with fiendish glee. "I am so, so funny!"

The young woman stared at him in disbelief.

"Speechless, my dear? Good. We don't have time to talk. I've got to go." He paused and smiled at his captive. "I'll be back in a little while, fair maiden. While I'm gone, think of me!"

Jamie heard him bar the door on the outside. The sound of the motorcycle's engine signalled his leaving.

Jamie sat for a moment, completely terrified. Her mind was frozen with shock. She thought if she moved or made the slightest sound, Chad would burst through the door.

Tears began to course down her cheeks.

"What am I going to do?" She struggled to get up, but promptly fell back against the wall. She started to weep uncontrollably. Suddenly, a memory pushed its way to the front of her mind. She could see herself in her backyard as a child. Her father was teaching her to ride a bike. Having fallen hard on the first try, six-year-old

Jamie lay crying on the lawn. Her father scooped her up and made her try again. "Don't give up, Jamie girl," Dad had said. "Keep trying."

Jamie forced back the tears. She took several deep breaths in an effort to calm herself.

"I've got to get out of here before he gets back," she whispered.

The young woman began to work frantically to undo the rope around her wrists. In his zoned state, Chad hadn't tied them too well. Her heart pounding in her ears, she finally pulled the knots loose.

"Come on, come on!" she pleaded, grabbing at the rope around her ankles. It was tied much tighter than the other rope. Her hands began to burn and bleed with effort. Jamie stopped and pulled herself upright. Hopping over to the kitchen area, she searched for and found an old knife. She sawed at the rope with the dull blade. Persistence prevailed, and she jumped to her feet.

Jamie scanned the cabin for a way out. She knew Braxton had barred the door. There was no way she could force it open. Her only alternatives were the small square windows. They pulled open easily enough, but they were boarded shut from the outside. Grabbing an iron poker from the fireplace, Jamie began pounding on the boards. They gave way, and she hoisted herself through the opening.

The cabin was completely surrounded by thick woods. There was scarcely space to park a car. Jamie headed for the narrow road that led up to the cabin. She stopped.

I can't go that way, she thought. *Chad may be back any minute.* She turned herself around and surveyed the area. Panic surged through her. Behind the cabin, the mountain continued its steep climb.

"There's no other way but to go down," she told herself. "I'll just have to go through the woods and steer clear of the road."

She bolted into a run. A myriad of branches plucked at her clothes. She shielded her face as best she could, but soon she was covered with scratches. She didn't care. Her only thought was to get as far away from the cabin as possible.

Her hair caught on the sweeping bough of a prickly bush. She stopped and pulled at it, cursing the length of her hair. Finally tearing herself loose, she continued her flight. Trees, branches, and leaves passed by her in a blur. A gnarled root clutched Jamie's foot, and she went tumbling to the ground.

I hate that, she thought, jumping up and dusting herself off. *It's just like in the movies. Terrified girl running from monster trips and falls, hurting her ankle. You yell at her to get up, you idiot.*

Jamie started to laugh and cry at the same time.

"I'm losing it," she said aloud. "Get a grip on yourself, Jamie. This is not a movie."

Shafts of sunlight flickered through the trees, creating patches of glowing green.

"Sun will be going down soon," Jamie said to herself. "I better get moving."

The young woman began to run again. The downward slope of the mountain seemed to go on forever. She ran until her side flared with painful cramps. Dropping to the ground, the young woman closed her eyes.

"Got to rest," she panted. "Got to rest." This time she let the tears come freely. Feelings of isolation and loneliness nearly suffocated her. Thoughts of her family stabbed her heart. She was miles and miles from love and help.

Finally her crying subsided. The sounds of the forest filled her ears. Tree frogs chirped and hummed incessantly. An occasional squirrel chattered noisily over some perennial feud. Birds called and sang, snatches of melody threading through the trees with a serendipitous harmony. Birds. Birds. What about them? Jamie lifted her head. Somebody had said something once about some kind of bird.

Sparrows, she remembered. *Reverend Jacobsen said God watches over the sparrows. And us. He watches us. He knows the hairs on our heads. He know and sees everything.*

Jamie sat up. Like a whisper quietly reverberating from ages past, the thought came: You are not alone. She closed her eyes and listened more intently to the birds. Maybe this stuff about God was not so crazy after all. She was beginning to feel peaceful for the first time in a long time. He sees me.

The baying of a hound ripped through the air. Startled, Jamie jumped to her feet. She was about to run when the dog crashed through the undergrowth. It barked and howled, insanely elated with its discovery. Jamie was so shocked by the dog that she failed to see the figure emerging from behind the trees.

"I had a feeling you might play hard to get," Chad Braxton mused from the other end of a rifle. "Tsk, tsk, don't you like me, fair maiden? Or are you being coy to arouse my passion?"

"Chad, you monster—"

"Now, now! No name-calling. That would bespoil your

beauty." He called the dog away. "How do you like my little helper? Snoozer is my dad's best hunting dog. Dad's things certainly come in handy," he said, patting the handle of the rifle. He stopped and looked furtively around, as if he thought someone might be nearby.

"Come on," he commanded, grabbing Jamie by the arm. "We've got to get back to the castle."

twenty

The farmhouse kitchen was full of people. Pastor Jacobsen and Louise sat beside Kate, praying silently with her. Billy was pacing the floor. Ben and Judah sat near the phone, waiting.

The jangle of the phone made everyone jump. Ben snatched the phone. "Watson?"

Ben listened to what the sheriff had to say and hung up. He shook his head and flopped down in a chair. "Nothing. Not a thing. Nobody's seen anything. Nobody here. Nobody in Lamberton. Nothing."

Judah stood up and looked out the back window. The sun would soon be setting. He looked out at the hills that graced the edges of the valley. A thought struck him.

"Maybe they're not in Lamberton."

All eyes were on Judah.

"Where would you hide out around here?" Judah asked.

Ben jumped up. "Somewhere in the hills, of course."

"But where could we possibly begin to search?" Billy asked. "We're surrounded by hills. They could be anywhere."

"Wait a second!" Ben pounded on the table. "Why didn't I think of that before? I've seen that Jeep! I've seen it! I was fishing. You know the eddy just below town, about five miles down River Road? I've been fishing over there for a couple weeks."

"Cut to the chase, Ben," prodded Judah.

"A couple times while I was there, I saw a green Jeep

drive by and turn up one of the old mountain roads."

"Which road?" asked Judah, his voice tense, his mind about to explode.

"The road that goes up to the old Fisher place, that hunting cabin."

Billy hurried to the phone. "I'm calling Watson."

"Wait a minute," cautioned Judah. "If they go driving up there in their cars, they'll scare Chad half to death. He might—" Judah caught Kate's eye and hesitated. "He might do something crazy. I know a better and quieter way. Shadow and I have been on that road a hundred times. Call Watson and tell him I'm going on ahead. Tell him to come, but no sirens."

Judah was out the door. In a matter of minutes, he was flying down the road, Shadow's legs a pounding blur of black.

Chad prepared the cocaine while Jamie watched. Time seemed to stand still, roaring in her ears.

"This stuff will take us to the moon!" Chad cried ecstatically.

Life is so fragile, Jamie thought. *There's got to be more. It can't just end like this. I'm going to die.* The thoughts turned over and over in her mind. Pictures of her mom and dad flashed across her mind. Maybe they're going to get a divorce. I guess that doesn't matter now. Nothing is ever certain. Then she thought of her grandmother. There was something certain about her. What was it? Jamie's mind was cloudy with fear and shock. What was it about Grandma that never changed? Oh yeah. Her faith. She never lost faith in God. Said so many times that God had never let her down. Even when Grandpa died.

"Jamie," Katie had spoken to her after John's death. "Sometimes I get mad at God for taking your grandpa first. But then I remember He's God, I'm not. He's here with me, I'm not alone. He'll never leave me or forsake me."

Not alone. Jamie remembered her feelings in the woods. *Oh, God*, she prayed in her heart, *please help me*. Words from Pastor Jacobsen began to permeate her mind like a forgotten song. "Don't be afraid of those who can kill the body," the pastor had said. "Fear God. What Christ gives is eternal, unchanging. Certain. That which is hidden will be revealed. In the hidden places of the heart we can experience God's love."

An image of the stained-glassed window in the church flashed in her mind. She could see the storm-tossed boat and the resolute Christ. The turmoil of the moment, the uncertainty of life swirled around Jamie like relentless waves. In the midst of clamoring insanity, the hidden need of her heart was laid bare. She saw a rock immovable, a passage out of the darkness and into the light. She saw Christ.

In the dimming light of the cabin, while a madman concocted a nightmare, Jamie Carrigan realized the truth of God's love. For the first time in her life, she called out to Christ, and God became her Father. In the power of that moment, the truth of His nearness struck her in the depths of her being.

"Eureka!" yelped Chad. "We're all set!" Holding a syringe, he walked over to Jamie. "I'm going to snort my snow but I know I can't make you snort it. So I'm going have to inject you. That way we can go over the edge together. Isn't that sweet?" Chad's entire body was shaking. His face was flushed. "Are you ready?"

Jamie looked into his eyes. "Why, Chad? Why are you doing this?"

A smile slowly spread across the young man's troubled face. "Because I love you, fair maiden. And you love me. And this way, we can be together always. I told you before, I always get what I want. And I want you. Now, hold still."

"He's here, you know," said Jamie. "He sees us."

Chad twirled around frantically looking for an intruder. "Who? Where is he?"

"You can't see Him. It's the Lord. He's here."

Chad shook his head and clucked his tongue. "I never would have guessed it, Jamie dear. You, of all people, grabbing on to faith in a crisis. That's such a cowardly and escapist thing to do, don't you think?"

Jamie looked into Chad's eyes. "What do you call what you're doing? Aren't you trying to escape? What are you escaping from, Chad?" she asked, trying to buy time.

"I'm not escaping," he snapped. "I just like living on the edge, that's all. Besides, nobody cares what I do. Everyone is so narrow-minded. They don't understand me. Nobody cares what I do."

"Your parents care about you, Chad."

"That doesn't count," he retorted, sweat dripping down his face. "They're my parents. They have to care."

"I care what happens to you," said Jamie softly.

"I know you do!" Chad hugged himself. "That's why I brought you here. So we could be together. I told you that already. Are you going deaf or something?"

"Chad, why don't we go down to the diner and get something to eat? We can talk things over. Maybe we could go over to your house and see your mom and dad."

"Go to the diner?" said Chad, his brow furrowed with thought. "Maybe we could, maybe. We could go to the movies, too." He stopped and slapped the side of his face. "Aha! You're just trying to confuse me. You're just stalling for time! I caught you in the act! Na, na, na, na, na," he sang in a sing-song voice. Chad wiped the sweat off his face with his sleeve. "No way, fair maiden. You can't fool me! I'm the master of trickery." He frowned. "Now hold still, I said. It's time for paradise!"

Jamie looked down at her hands and feet. Chad had tied her up again. As Chad bent toward her, she threw herself on the floor, screaming. She thrashed around as hard as she could.

"Stop it!" screeched Chad. "Stop it!" He ran over to the table and put down the syringe. He grabbed a cloth to gag Jamie. She tried to pull away from him. He slapped her hard across the face. It stunned her. "Jamie!" he hissed, putting his face next to hers. "Remember this?" He waved the pistol in front of her. "You mustn't be a naughty girl." His breath felt hot against her face. "You must be a good girl!" He tied the gag painfully tight.

Jamie was dazed. Chad leapt up to retrieve the syringe, when suddenly the front door smashed open. Without stopping, Judah threw his body against Chad. Chad went flying into the wall with a crash. He jumped to his feet and tried for the pistol on the table. Judah blocked Chad's arms with a powerful swipe, pushed Chad away, and grabbed the pistol himself. Chad lunged for Judah, but Judah dodged him. Braxton fell against the table and knocked it over. Powdered cocaine fell in a shower of white all over the floor. The syringe clattered down and rolled along the floor. Judah smashed it with his boot.

"No!" screamed Chad as he watched his dream scatter and fall between the rough-hewn boards of the wooden floor. He scrambled around, clutching at the elusive powder with trembling hands. "No, no." His voice trailed to a despairing whisper. He looked wearily at Jamie. "Now we can't go," he whined quietly. He sat on the floor and put his head in his hands. Judah watched as the man finally collapsed in a quivering heap.

"Jamie!" Judah cried. He rushed over and began to untie the gag. Jamie looked up at him, her eyes wide with shock and relief. She couldn't speak. Judah didn't wait to untie her but swept her into his arms. As he held Jamie close, he hid his face in her long brown hair. Jamie suddenly felt her hair getting wet with his tears. The man was weeping.

"Oh, dear God. Jamie. I almost lost you." he cried. He held her tighter as if he'd never let her go. Jamie felt the strength of the man's love coursing through his arms, flowing through his silent tears. She began to tremble with the realization that the nightmare was over.

"Very, very touching," Chad's voice slithered across the room. Jamie's heart leaped to her throat.

Judah instinctively grabbed the pistol and whipped around to face Braxton.

"Stalemate," said Chad gleefully. He was standing near the door with his father's rifle in hand. "You can't shoot me, because I'll shoot you. Sounds like a nursery rhyme, doesn't it?"

"What do you want?" Judah barked.

"How did you get up here so sneakily?" asked Chad. "Why?"

"Just answer me or I'll aim at the little pheasant you have there under your arm." He grinned at Jamie.

"Horse." Judah answered. "I came by horse."

Chad's eyes widened. "Fabulous! I'll just borrow your horse, if you don't mind. Where is it?"

"Out front," Judah replied.

Chad backed up to the door facing Judah and Jamie. He slowly opened it. "Now don't do anything rash!"

"Oh, we won't," muttered Judah under his breath, a gleam in his eyes.

Braxton slammed the door shut and found the horse next to the Jeep. He ran toward Shadow, reaching for the rein. Judah ran to the door in time to see Shadow promptly rear up and knock Chad to the ground. His rifle flew out of his hand into the grass. The agitated horse paced nearby, snorting angrily at the stranger.

Judah sprinted over and picked up the rifle. Chad didn't move. Shadow had knocked the wind out of him.

The sounds of car engines signalled the arrival of the police. Sheriff Watson and his men poured on their search lights. They jumped out of their cars, guns pulled and trained on Chad Braxton.

"I don't think you need the guns," Judah said quietly.

Watson looked at the man slumped over on the ground. He signalled his deputies, who hurried over and hand-cuffed Braxton. They pulled the man to his feet and led him to one of the squad cars.

The sheriff entered the cabin, scanning the scene.

"Are you all right, Miss Carrigan?" he asked.

Jamie nodded. "Do you think you could get these ropes off me sometime today?"

"Oh, yeah, I forgot," said Judah. He quickly untied

them. Jamie got up, rubbing her wrists. Looking around
the mess, her eyes fell on the broken syringe. She shuddered and turned away. "I want to go home."

"You can ride in one of the squad cars, Miss Carrigan.
John here will take you. I want to have a word with the
Lone Ranger here."

Jamie smiled at Judah. "Go easy on him, Mr. Watson.
He saved my life."

"See you at the house," said Judah.

The young policeman guided Jamie out the door. Watson
pointed a long finger at Judah. "What in blazes got into
you? You could have gotten yourself, and possibly Miss
Carrigan, killed! I ought to haul you in for interfering
with police work."

Judah simply nodded. "Yes. I guess you're right."

"We were handling it. You have no business interfering
with a police investigation."

"Yes, you're right."

"Riding a horse to the rescue. This isn't a cowboy
movie!"

"Right again."

"Well, just don't do it again."

"I promise."

twenty-one

As the squad car pulled into the King driveway, Kate and Ben burst out the front door of the house. They helped Jamie out of the car and practically carried her into the house. Katherine and Louise surrounded her, crying for joy. Billy and Ben started whooping and hollering. Pastor Jacobsen stood in the corner, grinning from ear to ear and praising the Lord. At the sight of such dear family and friends, Jamie let herself go. All the tension and terror of the day drained out of her in racking sobs.

The tears subsided. A deep sense of peace stirred in Jamie's heart. She knew it was from more than being safe.

"Oh, Grandma. So much has happened."

Kate saw the sparkle in her granddaughter's eyes. "I think I already know what you're going to say."

Jamie nodded. "You were right. Judah was right. Billy tried to tell me. It's real! God's love is real! Oh Grandma! It's like I've finally found my home. A home I'll never have to leave!" She looked over at the pastor. "And you, Reverend Jacobsen—your sermons. Your words reached me in the middle of the woods when I thought I was going to die." She leaned back on the green sofa. "I'm so grateful for all of you."

"And Toto, too?" Billy quipped. At that, everyone laughed. Jamie threw a pillow in his direction.

"I think we'd better take care of your face now, young lady," Ben said briskly. "We'd better clean up those

175

scratches and put some ice on the swelling."

"Yes, Dr. Wheelock, whatever you say," Jamie smiled.

"Jamie, I'm so glad you're okay," Ben said somberly. "I can't help but feel this is somehow my fault."

"Mr. Wheelock!" Jamie objected.

"Ben! Don't be ridiculous!" Kate exclaimed. "How could this possibly have anything to do with you!"

"Chad Braxton came into the shop for antihistamines starting in January. That's okay, it's winter time, cold and flu season. But then he kept coming. And it was always the same. I finally got a hunch that he was dabbling in drugs. Certain drugs cause nasal discomfort and congestion." Ben shook his head. "I should have said something to you, Jamie. I should have warned you."

Jamie reached out for Ben's hand. "Stop thinking that way. You know I probably wouldn't have listened to you, anyway."

"If it weren't for Ben, we may not have found Jamie in time," a voice said firmly from the living room door.

"Judah!" Everyone clapped and cheered and slapped him on the back. Judah grabbed Ben's hand and lifted it in a victory sign. The room was buzzing with joy.

Kate took the opportunity for some last-minute scheming. "Why don't we all go in the kitchen and whip up a meal for Judah and Jamie? They must be tired and hungry!"

Everyone took the hint, although Billy had to be dragged out by Pastor Jacobsen. Suddenly, the room was quiet. Judah and Jamie were alone. Jamie stood up and rushed into Judah's arms.

"Judah," she whispered. At last, she rested in his arms, knowing that it was where she belonged. She looked up into his rugged, honest face. "Thank you for praying for me. I found His love, Judah. It was just like you said. I really did find it. Or maybe He found me!" She laughed and hugged Judah tightly.

Judah's blue eyes were warm with love. "I told you so," he teased.

"And I discovered something else this summer."

"Oh?" His heart pounded, and Jamie felt him tremble. "What's that?" he asked huskily.

"I love you, Cowboy."

Judah breathed a deep sigh of relief.

"I love you too, Princess," he whispered. "But I think you know that."

Judah hesitated. Then he shyly leaned down and kissed Jamie gently on the lips. No tray clattered to the floor, no horn blared angrily, but the five people standing in the hallway did applaud. Even Billy Ritchfield.

"And on top of all that," Jamie whispered into Judah's ear, "Billy's going to be your best man."

Judah looked at her in surprise. Then he threw his hat in the air with a whoop.

"All right, all right, enough of that," Ben interrupted. "Jamie's face needs fixing. Now come on in the kitchen and sit down."

Jamie obeyed, and everyone stood around the table staring at her. They watched as Ben carefully cleaned her scratches and applied antiseptic. Kate prepared an ice pack for the swollen side of Jamie's face.

"He hit you, Jamie?" asked Billy. His voice was shaking with anger at the sight of her bruised cheek and eye. "If I ever get my hands on him, he'll regret the day he was born!"

"Billy!" admonished Kate. "Calm down. You're going to upset her."

"That's okay," responded Jamie. "But you know what? I feel sorry for Chad Braxton. If you could have seen him at the cabin, you'd feel sorry for him too. He was confused and messed up. He's lonely, and his brain is fried from drugs. It's a shame."

Judah nodded. "She's right, you know. I never thought I'd be saying this, but I feel sorry for him too. It makes me more thankful for what I have now."

"We'll put him on the prayer list," suggested Reverend Jacobsen.

"Well," spat Ben Wheelock. "You lovely, holy Christians can spout all the forgiveness you want! I'm mad as a wet hen, and I don't care who knows it!"

Jamie laughed at Ben's choice of words.

Kate put her hand on Ben's shoulder. "I'm mad too," she said. "But when I'm done being mad, I'll forgive the boy. But I'll tell who we're going to have to tie down when he gets here."

"Who?" asked Jamie, holding the pack over her eye.

"Your father. I called your parents when we first found out you were missing. They caught the first flight out here. Probably won't arrive until after midnight, though."

Jamie suddenly felt a little dizzy. "I think I better lie down," she said.

"Good idea," said Ben. "And I think everybody should clear out and let you rest."

"You're the boss," said Jamie. "By the way. Violet Cranberry came by the store today. Told me some interesting stories about you."

"Fiddlesticks," was all Ben would say.

"You should try to eat something," said Louise as she got ready to leave. She gave Jamie a kiss. "I'm so glad you're safe, dear."

Pastor Jacobsen nodded. "Ditto!" he said. "What a story we'll have to tell on Sunday morning!"

Jamie smiled. "Tell it all." She got up walked to the foyer.

"I don't want to go upstairs yet," she said. "I want to sit in the living room. Do you think we could have a fire in the fireplace?"

"I'll make it," Billy volunteered.

"I'll be going now," said Ben. "You take care of yourself, young lady."

Kate walked him to the door. "Thanks Ben," she said. "You saved Jamie's life when you remembered the Jeep. I will never tease you about your fishing again!" She slapped him on the back.

"Ouch!" Ben exclaimed. "I'm still sore, you know."

"I forgot! You'd better put more ice on that bump, Dr. Wheelock."

"All right, all right," said Ben, rubbing the back of his head. "And Kate, I guess there really is power in prayer, eh? Maybe there's hope for my poor old soul after all."

Kate laughed and shooed him out the door.

Billy had a fire blazing in the fireplace. Jamie sat on the couch, soaking in the warmth. Judah sat next to her with his arm around her.

"Best man," Billy muttered. "I'm always somebody's best man."

"You mean, like 'always the bridesmaid, never the bride'?" Jamie teased.

"Very funny," scowled Billy. He leaned back in the rocking chair and looked at Jamie. "Some day, I'll sweep the heroine off her feet, and it'll be time for paradise!"

Jamie looked at Billy. At the sound of his words, she suddenly saw Chad's face. It's time for paradise. Her hand flew to her throat and she began to tremble violently.

"Jamie! Are you all right?" asked Judah.

She shook her head. Her eyes filled with fear.

"He said he was going to take me to paradise. He was going to give me cocaine. He was going to kill me!" She bent over sobbing.

"Jamie, I'm sorry! I didn't mean to—" Billy pleaded.

"It's okay, Billy," said Judah. "She's still suffering from shock."

Kate hurried in from the kitchen. She sat down with her granddaughter and tried to soothe her. Jamie quieted down.

"We'd better go," said Judah to Billy.

"Yes, I better go before I say something stupid again."

"Come here, Billy Ritchfield," said Jamie. She signalled to him to come close. She kissed him on the cheek. "You're a great friend," she said. "The greatest."

Billy blushed and followed Judah out the door.

"Great friend," they heard him complain as he walked out the front door. "I'm always the great friend."

Just after midnight, Jamie's parents arrived and rushed in to assure themselves that she was all right. Dan Carrigan cursed every time he looked at his daughter's bruised face. Ellen sat holding Jamie's hand, tears running down her cheeks.

"You're safe, and that's all that matters," said Ellen.

"I'm okay, Dad. Stop staring at me."

"I'm sorry. I can't help it. When I think of that creep and what he tried to do—"

"Dan," Ellen implored him. "Jamie's had enough excitement for one day."

"Look," Jamie intervenes. "It's almost one o' clock. I'm going to bed. Can I sleep in your room tonight, Grandma? Just for tonight."

"Sure, dear. It's perfectly understandable. I'll go get your pillows."

Kate headed for the stairs, and Jamie got up to follow her. Dan gently took her arm.

"Just a minute, Jamie girl. There's something I want to say to you."

Jamie stopped and looked at her father. *Oh great*, she thought. *Of all the nights he picks to tell me he's leaving Mom, it has to be this night.*

"Sit down, Jamie."

She sat next to her mother. Ellen squeezed her daughter's hand.

"I know you've been worried about your mom and me. Things haven't been very good between us. In fact, they've been awful." He shoved his hands in his pockets. "I want you to know it was my fault. Your mom has been great. I just got real selfish and only thought about myself." He turned to look into his daughter's eyes.

"I almost lost her, Jamie," his voice broke. "I almost lost your mom. But I woke up, that's what I'm trying to tell you. I woke up, and I'm trying to make it up to her. And now this happens. I almost lost you." Tears coursed silently down the man's cheeks. "You sort of get things in perspective when your life falls apart. You figure out real quick what's important and what's not."

"I know," said Jamie.

He cleared his throat. "I'm trying to say I'm sorry." He looked at Ellen.

"Dan," she whispered. "I love you."

Jamie looked from one parent to the other. Her heart was bursting with relief and joy. But even as she looked at the two of them, she realized that the change in her own heart did not hinge on whether or not her parents reconciled, or whether or not she had been saved from Chad Braxton. Her heart would forever find its home in Christ, regardless of what life would bring.

Jamie got up and kissed her father on the cheek.

"Thanks, Dad," she said. "I'm glad things are working out. I was real worried. The Lord is so good to us."

Ellen's eyebrows shot up. "The Lord is good? That came out of our Jamie's mouth?"

Jamie smiled. "I'll tell you all about it tomorrow. I'm going to bed!"

epilogue

"Good morning, Violet. Can I help you with something?" Jamie gave the woman a knowing wink.

Violet giggled and nodded her head. "Yes, dear. You're not too busy, are you?" She lowered her voice. "Where's Ben?" she hissed.

"He's in the back," Jamie whispered back. "He probably doesn't even know you're here!"

"Good morning, Violet!" Ben called from the back of the store.

"Oh that man!" Violet scowled.

"Come on," said Jamie. "He won't even see us!"

Jamie and her accomplice handled their mission with speed. In a matter of minutes, Violet was on her way with her package.

"See you later, Violet!" yelled the pharmacist from behind his partition.

"Humph!" Miss Cranberry gave one last primp to her hair and stomped out the door.

"I'm impressed!" said Judah from his stool at the counter. "You're really good with people."

"She's a prize, all right," chimed in Ben. "I don't think I'm going to let you have her, Judah. After all, I saw her first."

"Want to arm wrestle for her?" inquired Judah. He put his elbow up on the counter. Ben eyed Judah's muscular arm.

"On second thought, I'll settle for being godfather to

your first kid. Deal?"

"Deal," said Judah with a grin.

"Hey, wait a minute, don't I have any say in this?" Jamie piped up.

"No," the two men spoke in unison.

Jamie shrugged. "I can't fight both of you. Hey, it's five o'clock. I feel like walking home today. Who wants to be my escort?"

"Not me," replied Ben. "Exercise is bad for my health."

"I guess it's up to me," said Judah. He held out his arm, and Jamie curled hers through it.

"See you later, Ben."

Judah and Jamie walked through town. The air was warm and sweet with the smell of newly mown hay. Jamie took a deep breath.

"That's my favorite smell," she said.

Judah looked over Jamie. The sunlight brought out the golden highlights in her brown hair. Her eyes were peaceful and happy. He stopped her at the turn off to Ryder Road. "You look beautiful," he said.

Jamie blushed and looked down the road that led to her grandmother's. The trees on either side of the road merged in a canopy of green. Shafts of light streaming through the trees scattered the road with gold.

"So will you?" Judah asked.

"Will I what?"

"Marry me."

"I don't know," teased Jamie. "I hear there's a wise old woman who lives down that path of gold. Maybe I should go ask her what she thinks."

"Let's go," smiled Judah. He clasped her hand tightly in his own.

Together they walked down the road toward Kate's home. Jamie couldn't help feeling that her time spent with her grandmother had been a road her heart had needed to travel. Like the contrasting light and shadows that pulsed beneath the canopy of leaves, Jamie's journey traced moments of brightness and profound darkness. At journey's end, she found her heart was where it always should have been. Hidden in the arms of her Creator.

As they approached the red mailbox, Jamie could see her grandmother inspecting her flowers in the front yard. She squeezed Judah's hand and kissed him gently on the cheek.

"I'm home," called Jamie to her grandmother. "I know," Katherine King called back to her granddaughter with a warm smile. "I know."

"I'll take that as a yes," shouted Judah.

The Delaware Valley resounded with the shout of the cowboy and the laughter of the princess. The wise, silver-haired woman looked on and smiled.

A Letter To Our Readers

Dear Reader:

In order that we might better contribute to your reading enjoyment, we would appreciate your taking a few minutes to respond to the following questions and return to:

Karen Carroll, Editor
Heartsong Presents
P.O. Box 719
Uhrichsville, Ohio 44683

1. Did you enjoy reading *Passage of the Heart*?
   ❏ Very much. I would like to see more books by this author!
   ❏ Moderately
   ❏ I would have enjoyed it more if

   _____

2. Where did you purchase this book?_____

   _____

3. What influenced your decision to purchase this book?
   ❏ Cover   ❏ Back cover copy
   ❏ Title   ❏ Friends
   ❏ Publicity   ❏ Other _____

4. Please rate the following elements from 1 (poor) to 10 (superior).
   - ❑ Heroine
   - ❑ Hero
   - ❑ Setting
   - ❑ Plot
   - ❑ Inspirational theme
   - ❑ Secondary characters

5. What settings would you like to see in Heartsong Presents Books?

   _____

   _____

6. What are some inspirational themes you would like to see treated in future books?

   _____

   _____

7. Would you be interested in reading other Heartsong Presents Books?
   - ❑ Very interested
   - ❑ Moderately interested
   - ❑ Not interested

8. Please indicate your age range:
   - ❑ Under 18
   - ❑ 18-24
   - ❑ 25-34
   - ❑ 35-45
   - ❑ 46-55
   - ❑ Over 55

Name _____

Occupation _____

Address _____

City _____ State _____ Zip _____

HAVE YOU MISSED ANY OF THESE TITLES?

These additional titles in our Romance Reader series contain two complete romance novels for the price of one. You'll enjoy hours of great inspirational reading. Published at $7.95 each, these titles are available through Heartsong Presents for $3.97 each.

_____ RR2 A MIGHTY FLAME &
        A CHANGE OF HEART by Irene Brand

_____ RR3 LEXI'S NATURE &
        TORI'S MASQUERADE by Eileen M. Berger

_____ RR5 SONG OF JOY &
        ECHOES OF LOVE by Elaine Schulte

_____ RR7 FOR LOVE ALONE &
        LOVE'S SWEET PROMISE by Susan Feldhake

_____ RR9 SUMMER'S WIND BLOWING &
        SPRING WATERS RUSHING by Susannah Hayden

_____ RR10 SECOND SPRING &
        THE KISS GOODBYE by Sally Laity

Great New Inspirational Fiction
from HEARTS♥NG PRESENTS
Biblical Novel Collection #1
by Lee Webber
Two complete inspirational novels in one volume.

_____ **BNC1 CALL ME SARAH**—Can Sarah, like Queen Esther
be used by God . . . even as a slave in Herod's place?
CAPERNAUM CENTURION—One Centurion's
life is irrevocably changed by his encounter with a
certain Nazarene.

Citrus County Mystery
Collection #1

by Mary Carpenter Reid
Two complete inspirational mystery and romance novels in one volume.

_____ **CCM1 TOPATOPA**—Can Alyson Kendricks make an historic
village come alive . . . without becoming history herself?
DRESSED FOR DANGER—Roxanne Shelton's
fashion designs were the key to her success . . . but
did they unlock a closet of secrets?

*BOTH COLLECTIONS ARE AVAILABLE FOR $3.97 EACH THROUGH
HEARTSONG PRESENTS. ORIGINALLY PUBLISHED AT $7.95 EACH.*

LOVE A GREAT LOVE STORY?
Introducing Heartsong Presents —
Your Inspirational Book Club

Heartsong Presents Christian romance reader's service will provide you with four never before published romance titles each month! In fact, your books will be mailed to you at the same time advance copies are sent to book reviewers. You'll preview each of these new and unabridged books before they are released to the general public.

These books are filled with the kind of stories you have been longing for—stories of courtship, chivalry, honor, and virtue. Strong characters and riveting plot lines will make you want to read on and on. Romance is not dead, and each of these romantic tales will remind you that Christian faith is still the vital ingredient in an intimate relationship filled with true love and honest devotion.

Sign up today to receive your first set. Send no money now. We'll bill you only $9.97 post-paid with your shipment. Then every month you'll automatically receive the latest four "hot off the press" titles for the same low post-paid price of $9.97. That's a savings of 50% off the $4.95 cover price. When you consider the exaggerated shipping charges of other book clubs, your savings are even greater!

THERE IS NO RISK—you may cancel at any time without obligation. And if you aren't completely satisfied with any selection, return it for an immediate refund.

TO JOIN, just complete the coupon below, mail it today, and get ready for hours of wholesome entertainment every month.

Now you can curl up, relax, and enjoy some great reading full of the warmhearted spirit of romance.

— — Curl up with Heart♥ng! — — —

YES! Sign me up for Heart♥ng!

FIRST SET TO SHIP OCTOBER 15, 1992.
Orders received after that date will be shipped immediately!
Send no money now. We'll bill you only $9.97 post-paid with your first shipment of four books.

NAME _____

ADDRESS _____

CITY _____ STATE / ZIP _____
MAIL TO: HEARTSONG / P.O. Box 719 Uhrichsville, Ohio 44683
YES